"I am not kind, *mademoiselle*."

"I can well believe it!" Sarah assured him sharply, stung by his hard reply. "However, as it doesn't concern me, I can afford to ignore it."

"So you bite back when bitten, *mademoiselle*?" Armand mused quietly. "I was beginning to imagine that you were merely a delicate English flower with little substance."

"The English rose has sharp thorns!"

Dear Reader,

I spend a lot of time in France and usually make sure that I stay in the sun. A few years ago, however, I found myself in Northern France almost by accident. I was lost!

The atmosphere of the small towns and villages was much more brooding than I had expected and the scenery and mood of the area stayed in my mind.

From that came the idea of a dark, brooding man, a man with a temper as uncertain as the northern weather.

In a way, too, the girl is lost because she has nothing to cling to until she finds that she can dare to dream about a man who is as strong as the land around him. And so *Tender Deceit* was born.... I hope you enjoy it!

Yours,

Patricia Wilson

TENDER DECEIT
Patricia Wilson

Harlequin Books

TORONTO • NEW YORK • LONDON
AMSTERDAM • PARIS • SYDNEY • HAMBURG
STOCKHOLM • ATHENS • TOKYO • MILAN
MADRID • WARSAW • BUDAPEST • AUCKLAND

ISBN 0-373-03364-8

TENDER DECEIT

Copyright © 1994 by Patricia Wilson.

First North American Publication 1995.

Printed in U.S.A.

CHAPTER ONE

'YOU are being impossible!'

The voice was deep, impatient and Céline Couvier glanced up with a mockingly pained expression on her face.

'I? Impossible? How am I impossible?'

The dark masculine eyes narrowed irritably as Armand Couvier looked down into his mother's face.

'You know perfectly well that you are planning to manipulate this girl for your own ends.'

'It is not for my own ends, Armand. I may be attempting to manipulate her but it is with the very best intentions. Besides, it was her father's last request and I could not in any circumstances deny him.'

'It seems to me that you have rarely denied him anything,' he murmured caustically and Céline smiled, an air of reminiscence about her.

'No, that is true. It lasted a very long time—twenty years to be exact. We cared deeply about each other, John and I.'

'But not enough to marry,' Armand said with a sceptical glance at her. 'To be someone's mistress for so long is, to my mind, peculiar and does not speak of caring.'

'There was no possibility of marriage. We were both already married.' Céline spoke with an air of finality and stood, smoothing her dress before looking back into the dark, watchful eyes. 'It is time you were going,' she stated firmly. Armand turned away impatiently, pacing about with an air of irritation that almost crackled through the room.

'Why I agreed to this I do not know,' he said savagely. 'To me the whole affair is disgraceful, unworthy of you. You are deliberately meddling with a life you know nothing of.'

'I know plenty about her life. She is going to need help and who is there to give it if I do not?'

'You do not know her!' he ground out, spinning to face her and fixing her with furious eyes. 'Perhaps this girl would not be so willing to come if she knew just how cunning you are and what you plan to do.'

'She has promised to come. She made a vow to her father and I telephoned her as soon as I received John's letter. He arranged everything before he died and I merely needed to know that she had agreed to come here. Also, you do not know what I plan to do, *chéri*.' Céline cast a flashing glance at her son. She was tenacious, determined to follow this through to the end, and in any case nothing intimidated her. 'I normally keep my mind to myself, my affairs also.'

'Affairs—yes! Certainly I did not know of this affair which seems to have gone on for most of my life.'

'It was not your business to know. You were a teenager, the time of life when it is easy to be shocked, easy, too, to be condemning. John and I were very discreet. It was not something we proclaimed to all and sundry. There was never any chance that we could marry. There was your father. I would never have divorced him, no matter what my feelings were. I married for life.'

Armand gave a cynical laugh and stood facing her, his hands in his pockets, his tall frame uncompromisingly masculine and tough, and Céline had the grace to look a little uneasy.

'Well, perhaps that is not the whole reason. There was you. Everything would finally come to you and I had not the slightest intention of having you lose any part of your inheritance merely because your father and I could not stand the sight of each other. I know what the law says, but I also knew your father. I knew how his mind worked. He would have had his lawyers come up with some clever way to hurt me and that could only have been through you. You would have lost something or been left with problems you could not solve. He was a man who would strike back from the grave by careful planning beforehand. I took no risks.'

'I find this distasteful,' Armand growled, his dark eyes beginning to take on the turbulent, stormy look that Céline knew well.

'You would not find it distasteful if you were in the same position yourself,' she pointed out sharply. 'Now hurry along, *chéri*. We do not want the girl standing about shivering, not knowing where she is about to go.'

'She would shiver even more if she knew what she is about to face,' Armand said acidly and his mother cast a long, amused glance at him, looking him up and down.

He was very tall and very dark, his hair thick and heavy around his head, beautifully cut. There was an enormous strength about Armand: wide shoulders tapering to lean hips and the long, strong legs now encased in jeans, the graceful hands now thrust into his pockets all added to a superb masculine elegance. He had the best of both worlds: the tough, unyielding stamina of his own people and, when he cared to use it, the easy *savoir-faire* of the Parisian. That of course was from his father. The two made a rather volatile mixture. His brooding good looks and the controlled animal power in all his movements would have drawn the attention of any woman but they would also fear him a little.

Céline smiled up at him rather smugly. She was very proud of her son. Dark eyes looked back at her with the questioning scepticism that was usually there.

'Do not attempt to involve me in your cunning plans,' he warned quietly. 'I have far too much to do with my time.'

'This I know.' Céline shrugged and moved her hands nonchalantly. 'I do not have any plan at all, as it happens. It is merely a matter of putting some distance between this girl and the man she is involved with in England. If I can persuade her to stay for a while, all will be well. If I cannot, *that* is when I shall need a plan. No doubt I will then call upon you to assist.'

'And you will be wasting your time. I object to all this and I am not much given to making plans about women,' Armand murmured dismissively, glancing at the thin gold watch on his wrist.

'Life runs smoothly for you because you drive it before you like a horse under the whip. You do not need plans. As to women, no doubt they fall over at your feet and beg to be walked on. For myself, I have always needed plans but as I have said I do not have a plan now.' She cast her eyes over him again. 'Are you not getting changed?'

'I *am* changed,' he assured her flatly. 'Clean, tidy and perfectly all right. I am merely a taxi driver in this.'

'I thought that perhaps you would wear a suit...'

'You thought wrongly.' The dark eyes narrowed in suspicion. 'I collect the girl dressed as I am or I do not collect her at all.' His narrow-eyed look probed for a second. Usually his mother was amusing, entertaining, but she did not have the normal attitude of mind for a woman of her age and when she was in this sort of mood he suspected her.

She saw the look on his face and knew it was pointless to argue. Armand had a mind of his own and when that mind was made up it was impossible to move it.

'Very well. I suppose you would turn the head of any woman, no matter what you were wearing. You are very handsome, Armand. I am always proud of you.'

Armand suddenly gave a harshly amused laugh, his black frown vanishing. 'Because people know then that I am your son?' he enquired mockingly.

'Handsome is from your father, *chéri*,' she informed him with a slight waspishness to her voice. She tapped her forehead delicately. 'Any cunning you have is from me.'

The dark eyes suddenly began to smile and he looked at her ruefully.

'I will go. But do not attempt to draw me into your plans. I am warning you for the last time, Céline.'

'Would I do that, Armand? Do I not always conduct my—affairs discreetly?' He raised one sceptical dark brow, his lips twisting in amusement and then he stepped to the door, leaving her behind.

Céline watched him from the window as he strode round to his car. Powerful and handsome with almost a feline grace to his movements, the frown back on his face, the wind tossing his thick hair, he was a man to be reckoned with. Had his father been alive now, he would not have found it so easy to cast ruthlessly aside the feelings of others. Armand would have dealt with him. He was a match for anyone.

'You are a handsome brute, *chéri*,' she murmured to herself. 'Sometimes I think, though, that, like your father, there is too much of the brute.'

All the same, she was smiling as she glanced round the warm kitchen. Whatever Armand thought, she had no plans at all. She was quite accustomed to thinking on her feet and although she had seen photographs of John's daughter she had really no idea what her character was like, except that she would probably be utterly spoiled. In any event, the girl would soon have more

money than was good for her and this man had her in
his clutches. If John had thought it then it was true.

Her eyes misted over but she straightened up and her
face took on a look of determination. John had wanted
this. He had given her a task that she would complete
to the very best of her ability. It was the last thing she
would ever be able to do for him. It would also give her
agile mind something to work at and she looked forward
to the time when Armand would return and bring into
her home the daughter of the man she had loved for
many, many years.

Armand drove away down the long, winding drive, his
eyes scanning the fields that were close to the château.
It was not a great, splendid place but it was quite spectacular none the less. It was dramatic, especially when,
as now, the dark storm clouds were gathered behind the
towers and the wind tossed the tops of the trees that
were close by.

There was the smell of rain in the air, rain that had
not yet come, and as he drove along he looked with satisfaction at the neat fencing, at the fields that were
already ploughed. There was a great deal to do and as
usual he had very little time. Tomorrow he would have
to get the men to work on the land nearer to the sea.
That was always the most difficult at this time of year
and if storms came it would have to be left.

His practised eye moved over the livestock that roamed
about at the lower end of the parkland and then he was
through the huge stone gates, gates topped by impressive
carved lions, and his car turned to the main road and
sped towards Paris.

A frown came back to the broodingly handsome face.
Why he was involving himself in this he did not know,
but one thing he did know: from now on, he had every
intention of keeping absolutely out of it. If the girl had

any sense, she would not have come. He wondered if she knew what her father had been to the woman she was soon to meet. She would have faced the same surprise he had faced himself when his mother had sprung this upon him yesterday.

He felt no disgust about that, in spite of his annoyance about his own particular mission. He knew perfectly well what sort of life Céline had lived with his father but he had had no idea that she had also lived a secret life, unknown to anyone. The long, carved lips twisted in amusement. If there was a game to play, Céline would play it. Even if she had married a poor man she would have been quite capable of living by her wits and her faculties were still as bright as they had ever been.

The English girl would have to have her wits about her too if she was not to be drawn into some sort of snare that his mother had planned, and Armand was sure that she had planned something, regardless of her airy words. Provided that he was not to be involved in any of this, Céline could do exactly as she wished. The château might not be huge but it was big enough for him to be able to keep out of their way while he was here. None of his time was going to be wasted on a girl who was probably spoiled and almost certainly deeply involved with someone who was altogether unsuitable.

He had some idea of how the very rich lived in England and John Thorpe had been one of the very rich. He was quite prepared to believe that this girl had been unchaperoned from an unsuitably early age. He wondered if this man was coming with her. Céline would not be pleased if she arrived with the man whose existence had led to this astonishing turn of events in tow.

He glanced at his watch again as he accelerated on to the motorway, the silver-grey car flashing along under his skilful hands. If he continued to dawdle along, considering matters which were not going to concern him, then the girl was certainly going to be left waiting in Paris. He made a low, disgruntled sound in his throat. All he had to do was identify her and deliver her to the château. The rest was up to Céline. It had absolutely nothing to do with him.

Paris was covered by the same threatening sky when he finally arrived and parked the car at the airport. The plane from London would already have landed; the formalities would be partially over. Far from being late, as far as he was concerned the timing was perfect. He did not wish to be hanging around and it was as cold and blustery in Paris as it was at home.

He strode into the building and looked about him, thinking with irritation that he was going to have trouble spotting this girl. He had no photograph. All he had was his mother's vague description. She was fair, Céline had said. *Mon Dieu*! The place seemed to be full of fair-haired people, most of them coming off the London plane.

He stood perfectly still, his hands in his pockets, his jacket pushed back. He would have to wait, wait until the area had cleared, if necessary, and then he would have to look for someone who was standing around too, waiting to be collected. No doubt she would have a haughty air about her; she was English, the daughter of a very wealthy man and no doubt accustomed to a great deal of attention. Armand was frustratedly aware that he was wasting valuable time here and as he looked round irritably his eyes fell on the girl he instinctively knew was the one he was seeking.

She was tall, slender and there was no mistaking the fair hair. It fell below her shoulders in a gleaming curtain, straight and heavy. A thick fringe across her forehead curved down around a face that was quite pale. She was looking slightly lost, obviously waiting for someone, and he could only think that she was waiting for him.

He observed her for a moment, trying to sum her up. She looked more alarmed than haughty, slightly bewildered, and this took him by surprise. This girl had probably travelled all over the world with her father; surely an airport would not bewilder her? He remembered then that it was only two weeks since her father had died. They had been very close, according to Céline, and he wondered if this was as much a surprise to her as it had been to him. Had her father confided in her long ago? It seemed unlikely; even now, again according to his mother, this girl was still only twenty-three.

She was, as he had expected, beautifully dressed. She was wearing a dark, richly blue suit that was a very sharp contrast to the pale fairness of her hair. The suit had a small white collar and the white near her face seemed to make her skin glow. Her eyes were almond-shaped. From here he could not see the colour but certainly they were not dark eyes like his own. He watched her for a few moments more and as she glanced at him uneasily he decided that it would be best to approach her, otherwise they would be standing here all day.

His lips tightened in annoyance. The girl was not exactly as he had imagined her. There was a rather delicate beauty about her, not something he would have expected to find in somebody who had managed to get herself involved with a man who had a bad reputation. Perhaps John Thorpe had been mistaken, or even jealous as this was his only child? Céline would have taken the word of John Thorpe without hesitation and it was quite possible that this girl had been forced here for nothing. It was more than likely, however, that her delicate beauty hid a mind like a voracious wasp. This was the very last time he would be involved in anything that Céline had planned.

* * *

Sarah stood with her luggage and looked round at the sea of faces. She sincerely hoped that someone would come to meet her as the woman had promised. It was impossible to be anything but nervous and she wondered if anyone else had ever faced a situation quite like the one she faced now. She gave a little sigh, biting into her lip and glancing again across the crowded area. The past two weeks had been shattering and her father's final revelations had left her almost numb inside. In spite of the shock she had made a vow that she was now obliged to keep and nothing would prevent her from honouring her word to her father.

She had to admit, though, that she felt alarmed, robbed of vitality, almost sick inside. That last day with her father had left her stunned. She had known that he was dying but she'd had no idea what he was going to tell her; she could still not believe it entirely. To think that all this time, since she was little more than a baby, he had lived two lives. Now she would have to face the woman who had been closer to him than anyone and she had really no idea how to act in the circumstances.

Her argument with Craig hadn't helped either. She had been upset by his attitude. As far as he was concerned her father was gone and no sort of promise would bring him back. Craig had wanted her to forget the whole thing and ignore the trip to France but Sarah had been adamant. The promise would be kept, no matter what her fears, no matter what the outcome. Her father had loved her. If he had also loved this woman then he had a good reason for his request.

All the same, she did not like quarrelling with Craig and she knew that lately she had relied a little too much on him. He wanted their relationship to grow but Sarah did not. She was fond of him but sometimes his way of life worried her. In any case, the mysterious spark of feeling was missing. She had never felt a spark of feeling with any man but feminine instinct alone told her it should be there, otherwise marriage would be like a complicated business deal.

Sarah brought her mind back to the present with a snap as she realised that a man was staring at her, watching her intently. She glanced away hurriedly but her gaze was drawn back to him almost at once and she felt curiously defenceless because he seemed to be dissecting her coldly.

He was tall, powerful-looking, sure of himself and he was unusual. There was no suave air of confidence that some of the men she knew had in plenty. His confidence was physical and mental, hard and very real, like an animal in peak condition, trained to kill. He wore blue jeans and a high-necked white sweater with a grey sports jacket and, even though he was casually dressed, he managed to make the whole outfit look surprisingly elegant. She was quite accustomed to seeing elegant men but this man was alarmingly different.

Sarah looked away from the brooding power of his gaze, feeling she had made some sort of escape but, even so, the dark eyes and the thick hair that swept across his forehead lingered in her mind as if she had been branded. She felt frighteningly disturbed and she had no idea why he was staring at her like that. She had never been looked at before with such intent, stormy irritation.

She glanced up again because she couldn't help doing so and his lips suddenly tightened grimly, the brooding eyes narrowing and lancing over her swiftly. Her heart simply took off at racing speed and gave an alarming little extra skip as he frowned even more and came striding towards her.

There was no mistaking his destination because his eyes never left her, and a sinking dread grew as he approached. Surely this was not the person who was meeting her? She prayed he was not but her hopes were dashed as he stopped in front of her.

'Mademoiselle Thorpe?'

'Yes.' Sarah felt breathless, tensing up at the sound of his harshly dark voice and he reached down for her luggage without looking at her again.

'I am Armand Couvier, *mademoiselle*. I have come to take you to the château.'

He swept up her luggage in an effortless way that spoke of great strength and Sarah followed him to the exit, her mind tensed with alarm because the situation was now more ominous than bewildering. Château? No château had been mentioned! No actual place had been spoken of but she had understood that she would be near Paris. Perhaps the château was near by, but now she was more than uneasy. How could she have been so stupid as to come here without demanding to know an address?

The name was correct. Madame Couvier had spoken to her on the telephone, not for long, merely to see if she was prepared to fulfil her promise to her father, and, when she had agreed, the woman had said that her son would meet her in Paris. It was all the contact there had been and she now felt that she had been foolish to put herself into the hands of this dark and alarming man who was escorting her out into a stormy afternoon. If he had noticed her vulnerability she was perhaps an easy prey.

He said nothing but the sight of his car was somehow very comforting—at least that was real and, at the moment, Sarah felt that she was drowning in unreality, her feet barely on the ground. The past two weeks had brought the feeling and this meeting had done nothing to ease it away. She felt numb with grief and shock, incapable for the moment of asserting herself and if this man was about to kidnap her she would be quite unable to struggle.

When her luggage was safely stowed he opened the passenger door for her, his manner coldly polite, the dark eyes silently and cynically summing her up, and soon the car swept speedily from the airport, out on to the motorway, driving her away from Paris and her last contact with any sort of security. Even in the hubbub and clamour of the traffic, there seemed to be a sort of menace in the atmosphere inside the car and as the airport was left behind the atmosphere simply grew.

After a few miles it became apparent that he was not about to speak at all and, although Sarah was still a little scared, her fright began to be tinged with annoyance. She had not asked for any of this. She had not demanded to meet Madame Couvier; it had been a promise to obey her father's wishes. She had not asked this dark, disturbing man to pick her up; it was some arrangement her father had made with his mother. All the same, she felt she had to break the silence. She was going to face a woman she had never seen before. It would be uncomfortable, perhaps embarrassing, and if she could speak to Armand Couvier in some civil manner before she got there she would not feel quite so alone.

Sarah made herself speak, half expecting that he would not reply as she was not altogether certain that he was human.

'Do we have far to go, *monsieur*?'

'Quite a way. I am afraid we do not live close to the glamour of Paris.' He made no attempt to take up her tentative offer of conversation and Sarah tried again.

'It looks as if there's going to be a storm,' she pointed out, leaning forward to gaze at the sky through the windscreen and he made a slight sound of irritation.

'It is not the best of times to visit the north of France. As in England, we are subject to the vagaries of the weather at this time of the year. You know the north of France, *mademoiselle*?'

'No.' Sarah glanced at him hopefully. He had perhaps decided to speak to her normally. 'I only know the south of France.'

She saw his lips twist sceptically and Sarah felt angry that she had even bothered to speak at all. No doubt he thought she spent her time on the Riviera, sunning herself, gambling and generally wasting her days away. A man like that would make his mind up without caring much about hard facts.

'I'm sorry that it was necessary for you to collect me, *monsieur*,' she stated stiffly. 'Of course, you are not involved in this.'

'I am doing this for my mother. She asked me to collect you and I agreed.'

His voice was abrupt, dismissive and Sarah glanced at the strong hands on the wheel. They were lean, tanned, long-fingered, almost graceful, but they looked uncompromising, just like their owner.

'I am grateful, *monsieur*. However, I only meant that you are not under any obligation.'

'And you have an obligation, *mademoiselle*?'

'A promise, *monsieur*. A promise I have to keep. A promise I think your mother is keeping also.'

'Why?' he asked in a hostile voice, his dark eyes on the road. 'Why is this promise so necessary to you?'

'My father asked me to meet his . . .'

'His mistress,' Armand assisted coldly and flatly. 'That is what she was, for many, many years.'

'I know. My father asked me to come here and—and stay for a month.'

'A month?' That gained his astonished attention and he shot an alarming glance at her before murmuring, 'She did not tell me this. My mother says only what she wishes to say. Until yesterday I did not know of this liaison. You are not going to some comfortable hotel where you will be ignored, *mademoiselle*. My mother is

a determined woman. You are prepared to stay for that
length of time with someone you do not know?'

'I must,' Sarah told him quietly although her heart
sank even further. She used the same firmly certain tones
she had used with Craig. Craig had been hostile about
this too, but for very different reasons. 'I'll keep my
promise, although it will be very difficult. I don't really
have the time.'

He *did* look sceptical then and he glanced at her again,
with an ironical look on his face, before he accelerated
to the fast pace of driving that seemed to be his normal
speed.

'And what do you do with your precious time,
mademoiselle?' he asked drily.

'I have a job, *monsieur*, which has been neglected since
my father began to be ill.' She sighed and turned away,
looking out of the window. Ahead of the car there were
obvious signs of approaching rain. Already it was darkening steadily and it made things more gloomy and miserable than ever, especially with such an unsympathetic
man beside her.

'A job, *mademoiselle*?'

Sarah could hear the derision in his voice, the sort of
thing she heard from anyone when she mentioned a job.
Her father had been wealthy, too rich for her to have to
work, and it irritated her to think that people assumed
that she would therefore not want to work.

'I have a shop,' she said sharply.

'A shop?' Sarah could see that she had almost
managed to startle him out of superiority. 'What sort
of a shop?'

'A bookshop, *monsieur*. At the moment it is very small
but I intend it to grow.'

'Ah! You want a big, thriving business, *natu-
rellement*!' There was a scornful certainty in his statement
and Sarah could see that she was already written off as

a grasping, greedy female with an eye for pleasure and a taste for money. He was another of these people who saw no further than the end of their interfering noses.

'No. I merely wish to handle more books!' Acidly, sweet derision came into her own tone and his lips twisted wryly. Sarah could see that it was an acknowledgement that he had been deliberately goading her. For some reason, taunting her was giving him pleasure and she could not understand why, unless he normally took his annoyance out on the nearest person to hand.

'I would have thought, *mademoiselle*, that you would have had some sort of profession, after university.'

'I did not go to university. I had no desire to. It is not obligatory in England to attend university. Those who decide not to go are never punished and rarely imprisoned. I wished to have a business of my own, to spend my life with books. That is what I do.'

She could almost feel his reluctant smile at her admonishing tone but she didn't care. He had annoyed her and she was not a simpering weakling. If he wanted answers to his questions he would have to make the best of the answers she chose to give.

'So you have left this business closed, *mademoiselle*?' His voice was not so harsh now but it was still like silk over steel and Sarah had grown tired of the verbal skirmishing.

'No. A friend is looking after it; a girl I went to school with. She has the same interests and I'm quite happy about leaving her in charge, although it has been quite a long time now.' She sighed and turned away to look out of the window. 'When my father was ill, I stayed with him.'

It had begun to rain, lightly at first over the past few miles but now with increasing heaviness and Sarah was very much aware of being locked in a speeding car with a dark, turbulent stranger, a man who for some reason disliked her although he did not know her at all. She could almost feel dislike and disapproval radiating from him and she hoped she would not have to see a great deal of him during the time she was at this château with his mother. She felt tired, dispirited and lonely.

'Is it very much further north, *monsieur*?' Again she felt the need to break the rather disturbing silence as they continued northwards and she got the same sardonic tone.

'Very far. We are northern peasants, my mother and I.'

Sarah's temper flashed and she decided to keep quiet from then on. If he couldn't be civilised she saw no reason why she should accommodate him in any way. She sat back in her seat, folded her hands in her lap and determined to say nothing more. She preferred to be lonely if the alternative was to be goaded.

If he wished for conversation he would have to make it himself. Certainly she was not prepared to make any further effort and she was well aware that if she had not made an effort in the first place he would not have spoken to her from the moment he had introduced himself.

There was something about him that made her refrain from thinking of him as uncouth; his peculiar sophistication and elegance was too real for that. But nevertheless his stormy darkness and his ill-concealed contempt made her realise that he was a man who would say anything he wished if a thought came into his mind and she suspected that in any circumstances he would do as he wished, regardless of other people's feelings.

CHAPTER TWO

IT WAS almost dark before Armand turned off the motorway. Sarah was tired, thirsty and, to her astonishment, quite hungry. She had been so nervous that she hadn't been able to eat before she left, telling herself that when she arrived in Paris she would have a snack. She had not had time and in any case the nerves had still been there and now she was feeling the need to eat. She hoped that Madame Couvier would be a little more civilised than her son. If he had been civilised at all he would have enquired if she wanted something to eat or drink, but he had not.

Her rather angry thoughts were suddenly stilled as she realised that they were going along country roads, tall trees at each side, and alarm came back, squashing her anger. She was very much aware again that she was beside a rather merciless man who for no reason at all thought very little of her and for a faltering moment she wished she had asked Craig to come with her.

Of course, he would have refused. He would not leave London and in any case it would have been quite unforgivable to bring Craig here to the house of complete strangers. She had the certain feeling that it would have infuriated Armand Couvier to murderous heights. Her own presence seemed to be infuriating him, although he had been expecting her, and Craig was so different from this dark, brooding Frenchman that there would probably have been great trouble.

The road began to climb and they were in more open country. In the distance she could see the dark outlines of a château, standing against the sky. It was not very large, not one of the glittering, astounding places she had seen on her visits to the south of the country, but it was strangely impelling none the less, aloof, almost ageless.

As they came closer there was still enough light for her to see it. It was grey, with long windows and towers that ended in steeply tiled roofs. Behind it were dark trees tossing in the approaching storm, black clouds gathering and a chill ran over Sarah's skin because she knew, without doubt, that this was the place where she had promised to stay for four long weeks.

She could see lights in the windows but they did nothing to give her a feeling of confidence and when the car swept in between tall, grand gates and travelled on a long drive through darkening parkland Sarah clasped her hands together more tightly still. She had arrived and she was about to see the mysterious woman she had known nothing of for the whole of her life, a woman her father had shared his love with. A woman he had kept as a secret from her for twenty years.

'We have arrived, *mademoiselle*.'

Sarah almost jumped at the sound of Armand's voice and she realised that the car had come to a halt before the château. She looked up the long, shallow flight of steps to the huge front door and she somehow did not think that there would be a welcome here. Madame Couvier was also fulfilling an obligation. *That* they had in common but she had nothing in common with the man who sat beside her.

She felt impelled to glance towards him and found that he was sitting staring at her, his arm along the back of the seat.

'A month is a very long time, Mademoiselle Thorpe,' he observed quietly. 'It will be lonely and I suspect that you are not accustomed to that. There is very little here to entertain anyone who is used to the bright lights of London. I sincerely hope you understand what your impetuous promise has brought you to.'

'My promise was not made impetuously.' Sarah's dark blue eyes stared into his own, refusing to look away in spite of her alarm. 'It was a shock to me and not something I am doing gladly. But my father was dying and I loved him. He wanted this and it is what I will do, no matter what the consequences.'

For a minute he continued to look at her, his dark eyes moving slowly over her pale face, and then he nodded, turning away.

'Yes, you probably will,' he murmured softly.

Sarah hadn't the faintest idea what he meant by that but no doubt it was some sardonic thought that was running through his mind. It seemed that even at the last minute he was trying to get her to change her mind and she was quite certain that if she did he would happily take her back to Paris without even opening the great door of the château. Her lips tightened angrily and she turned to the door, beginning to get out.

'*Un moment, mademoiselle*!' Armand got out of the car, coming round to help her and Sarah felt a flare of unease at the touch of the strong hand that came to her arm. Beneath her jacket, her skin shrank away from him as if her body recognised danger with no aid from her intellect, another sense to protect her. It was disquieting, especially as she was so very much aware of his dark hostility. He was not a man to be dismissed from the mind. She looked up at the towering château and the tossing trees blackly outlined against the sky. Heavy clouds were now piling up from the north, massing closer, and somehow they reminded her of Armand Couvier. She shivered in the cold wind, glancing at him anxiously.

'Come inside, *mademoiselle*.' This time, the derision was edged with amusement as his lips quirked and Sarah had the uneasy feeling that he had picked up her anxious, wavering thoughts. 'For all its looks, the château is warm and civilised,' he continued. 'We will get you inside where you can meet Céline, *n'est-ce pas*?'

'Céline? You call your mother that?'

'My mother does not stand much upon ceremony, as you can perhaps imagine, now that you have the facts at your disposal. She was your father's mistress for many years and she is extremely proud of the fact. You will find her a most—unusual woman.'

Sarah took a deep breath and went up the steps to the heavy front door as he urged her forward. No doubt Céline Couvier would be an unusual woman if she was anything like her son, and he certainly didn't stand upon ceremony. He didn't even think it necessary to speak, and when he did speak it was with either a faintly reprimanding air that left her feeling angry and frustrated or with amused and sardonic tolerance, as if she were a slightly disobedient child. He had deliberately tried just then to shock her, too. Well, he hadn't! She had already faced her shocks and they had left her so numb inside that any more would simply drift over her.

Armand opened the door and she stepped into the light, hearing the huge door close firmly behind her. It was a heavy, forbidding sound and in that moment she felt that everything of her past was suddenly cut off. It was an intangible, frightening feeling, as if she would be obliged to start a new life and the old one would fade into shadowy dreams. She felt an overwhelming urge to rush to the door and open it to the threatening storm but she bit down on her lip and straightened her shoulders. It was Armand Couvier and the odd effect he had on her. She was in danger of allowing him to intimidate her and she would fight the feeling.

The hall was paved with great flagstones and to her astonishment there was an extremely large Aubusson carpet in the middle of it, dark tables placed artistically against the walls with expensive-looking ornaments on each one. The staircase in front of her was also stone, mounting upwards spectacularly and curving at the top out of sight.

The place was bigger than Sarah had imagined from outside. Above her were two large, glittering chandeliers and she was sufficiently impressed to stare up at them. Armand had remarked drily that they were northern peasants and she could see now that his remark had been merely another taunt. She was nervously aware that he stood beside her, deliberately letting her gaze around. No doubt he wanted to impress on her that it was isolated and more than slightly alarming. He could have saved himself the trouble; she already knew that and she felt only relief as a door at the side of the hall opened and a tall, slim woman came out to meet her.

Céline Couvier was not exactly beautiful but she was certainly very attractive. The hair that had once been dark was now greying but it was arranged round her head in a way that told Sarah that this was a woman who was well-used to fashion. She wore a deep red caftan glittering with gold thread, she was wearing quite a lot of jewellery and there was more the look of the *Parisienne* about her than that of a woman from this dark northern climate.

She was not exactly what Sarah had imagined and at the moment she could not quite understand what her father had seen in this woman, although there was an air about her that was somewhat unusual, but then, the two of them had grown older together and in her youth Céline Couvier must have been strikingly good-looking.

Whether it was the look in her eyes or whether it was her ready smile and the wry assessment on Céline's face

Sarah could not tell, but she began to relax with the warm, dark eyes on her although she was still very much aware of the towering, stormy presence of Armand Couvier at her side.

'I have brought Mademoiselle Thorpe, Céline.' His voice seemed to reach inside Sarah, almost making her shiver, but Céline Couvier came forward, her hands outstretched.

'*Mademoiselle*, you are very welcome here,' Céline said quietly. 'I hope you will not be upset when I tell you that John spoke of you often. However you feel about things, *ma chère*, it is a fact of life. We are both bound by a promise and I hope you will stay.'

'I intend to stay, *madame*,' Sarah said determinedly. Now that she had seen this woman who had meant so much to her father, she felt that it might just be possible to survive here, providing that Armand kept well out of her way, because she knew she would never stop feeling uneasy with him. She also knew that his hostility would not ease at all. He disliked her for no reason, as far as she could tell.

To her relief, he turned and left, going out to the car to fetch her luggage, and Céline called after him that dinner would be ready very quickly and then, to Sarah's surprise, she led her into the kitchen.

'You are probably thirsty and hungry. The hunger we will deal with at dinner, but first of all a drink. I have made tea in your honour but I do not know if it is good, although I made it well enough for your father for a very long time.'

Sarah could see that Céline was being forthright from the very beginning to spare both of them embarrassment and she was grateful. She was also grateful for the thoughtfulness that had provided her with a drink. Tea was exactly what she needed right now. Armand would have let her starve and die of thirst, no doubt. For the moment he was well out of her sight and she was grateful for that too.

The kitchen was huge in the manner of an old French farmhouse. There were darkened beams and the walls were rough-hewn stone. Even so, there was a warmth and cosiness about the place that made Sarah feel instantly at ease. As Madame Couvier poured tea for her, Sarah glanced around appreciatively, only nodding vaguely when asked if she took milk and sugar.

The room looked as if it served several purposes. It had an air of being lived in. It was true that there were many gleaming electrical appliances discreetly placed against the stone walls but there was a fire burning brightly in a large fireplace, its light flickering across the room. Beside the fire there were two comfortable-looking armchairs and Sarah could see that somebody spent a great deal of time in this room.

As in the hall, the floor was flagged and there was a scattering of brilliant rugs. A large wooden table stood in the middle of the room with chairs around it, books partially lined one wall and there were a few bright pictures bringing more colour to the very old stone. Everywhere there was the sweet smell of herbs in the air, of spices and onions, and Sarah found it delightful. She looked up to find Madame Couvier watching her with amused eyes.

'The tea is to your liking, *mademoiselle*?'

'Perfect, thank you. Exactly as I like it. This room is perfect too. It is a comfortable room, *madame*.'

'Ah! That is because it is my domain. After all, I spend much of my time here so certainly I have it exactly as I want it. I do all the cooking.'

Sarah looked up in surprise.

'You don't have servants, *madame*?' As soon as she had said it Sarah wished the words back and she was very glad that Armand was not there. No doubt he would have taken it as an opportunity for some sardonic remark about her father's wealth, imagining probably that she lived in a house full of servants and was incapable of lifting a finger to help herself.

'There are two women who come in every day. The place is very big,' Madame Couvier said, 'and of course I could not manage it myself. There are two small cottages on the estate for the men who work on the land. At the moment we have five men. Three of them are from the village and two live in the cottages with their wives. Their wives come here to clean and assist me. There is always lots to do here but I am very content.'

Sarah nodded and sipped her tea. There was something about Céline Couvier that she found appealing. She was warm and although at the moment she was quiet Sarah had the feeling that she would be a very lively woman. There was an amused look in her eyes.

'No doubt, *mademoiselle*, Armand will have taken your suitcases to your room,' Céline said. 'As soon as you have finished your tea, you would perhaps like to go up there? I will be serving dinner in about half an hour. It will give you a little time to yourself after your journey.'

'Thank you, *madame*.' Sarah hesitated a moment and then came to a decision. If she was to stay here for four weeks she certainly could not go on with this formality; it would make life quite impossible. There was no doubt about it that Armand would continue to call her *mademoiselle* in his cold and stony way, but she had a feeling that she would be able to like this woman. For her father's sake she must at least try.

'I would be very happy if you would call me Sarah,' she said hesitantly.

She could see at once the pleasure that this gave to Céline because she smiled brilliantly and almost visibly relaxed.

'That would be wonderful, *ma chère*,' she said softly, 'and perhaps you could call me Céline? Even Armand calls me Céline.'

'I know. At the moment…well, perhaps later I can…'

'I know, I know,' Céline said comfortably, her amusement growing. 'At the moment you prefer to call me *madame*, in deference to my age.'

'Oh, *madame*! I didn't mean…'

'I am teasing, Sarah. Call me Céline whenever you feel that you can. I know that at the moment you must have some misgivings about me, perhaps some resentment. After all, I knew your father when your mother was still with him, but I would like you to know that I didn't in any way cause——'

'I have no resentment towards you, *madame*,' Sarah interrupted quietly. She had taken another decision. She had no desire to talk about her life but there were things that must be said if they were to feel comfortable with each other. Céline probably knew most of the things in any case. 'I know what you meant to my father and perhaps you know what happened as far as my mother was concerned. She left us when I was ten years old and never tried to see me afterwards. I know now that you have been my father's—friend since I was three and for seven of those years he was, to all intents and purposes, married but…when she left…in many ways it was a relief. You see, I remember her. She was cold, unloving. Many times as a child I would have liked to be loved, to be cuddled. With my mother I did not dare and I suppose my father had no more love than I had. At the time I didn't think of it. I thought only of myself. No, *madame*, there is no resentment. He deserved happiness and, from the way he spoke of you, I think you gave it.'

There were tears in Céline's eyes. She blinked them away rapidly but they had come very readily and Sarah was glad she had spoken. A slight noise behind her made her turn her head sharply, though, and Armand was standing there, looking at her intently. How much of the conversation he had heard she did not know, but her face flushed with embarrassment. Somehow it was perfectly all right to speak to Céline like that. It was not perfectly all right for Armand to hear. She didn't want him to know a thing about her. With him, it would be necessary to protect herself.

For another moment, his eyes met hers and Céline dried her eyes but not before she had patted Sarah's hand. Whether it was a comforting gesture for herself or for Sarah, Sarah did not know. There was an awkward silence for a moment and then Armand said, 'If you have finished your tea, *mademoiselle*, I will show you to your room. Perhaps you will wish to get ready for dinner, although we do not make a fuss of the event.'

'Tonight we do, Armand!' Céline had recovered and she turned to Armand with flashing eyes. 'It is Sarah's first night in the house and she is a very welcome guest. I will serve dinner in the small dining-room. It is warm in there, cheerful.'

'As you wish, Céline.' The derisive smile was back on Armand's face and Sarah hastily finished her tea before following him out into the flagged hall.

She wished he had not heard anything she had said. She had a great desire to keep well away from him, to be secretive. As far as she was concerned, he was not involved in this. He had performed his function in fetching her from Paris and possibly he would be the one who would take her back, but that was all.

She knew he was antagonistic towards her but, in spite of anything he may think, she was not a person who liked to fight. She liked and even needed tranquillity and there would be none of that with Armand Couvier around.

'This way, *mademoiselle.*'

He led her through the hall, alight with the glittering chandeliers, and up the great curving stone staircase, and Sarah walked behind him, trying to keep her eyes from the lithe, powerful way he moved. More and more she was realising how tall he was, how strong he looked and although there was not one spare ounce of flesh on him he looked capable of lifting her with one hand.

She swallowed uneasily at her own wild thoughts and was relieved to see, when they reached the top of the stairs, that the two long passages facing her, one going in each direction, were also very well-lit. It would be easy to become nervous in this house and she would have preferred to be in the warm, cosy kitchen now with Céline, instead of walking along beside a man who was as brooding as the storm that was approaching outside. She could hear the thunder rumbling in the distance and knew it would not be long before the storm broke over the tall rooftops of the château.

Her room was halfway along the passage and as Armand opened the door and Sarah stepped inside she was very pleasantly surprised. Her suitcases were on the luggage stool at the end of the bed and it was a great relief to find that she had a comfortable place of her own, a place she could retreat to if things in the château became impossible.

The room appeared to be furnished with French antiques, everything beautifully cared for. There was the lavender smell of polish in the air and, although she could see no sign of it, there was certainly some form of central heating because the room was comfortably warm. One of the long windows she had seen as she approached the château was set in the middle of the wall that faced the park and it was draped in thick curtains with beautifully glowing colours. Once again, Sarah realised that Céline had a great deal of taste. Everything she had seen so far fitted in beautifully with the place.

She was very anxious for Armand to leave but he strode into the room and opened a door at the side.

'Your bathroom, *mademoiselle*.'

That was another surprise. She certainly had not expected an *en-suite* bathroom in a place like this, but then, the château had obviously been very tastefully modernised.

'Thank you.' She expected him to go immediately and she began to unbutton her jacket, only to look up and find him still standing there.

'You think you will be comfortable here?' he asked quietly, his eyes holding her startled gaze.

'Oh, yes, thank you. I'm sure I will. I seem to have everything I need.'

'Let us hope so. Four weeks is a long time if you are uneasy.' The dark eyes ran slowly over her, narrowed and assessing as he inspected her from head to foot and Sarah's fingers stopped in their action of unfastening her jacket. He was disturbing her as nobody else had ever done. Beneath her clothes, her skin seemed to be flushing with heat and she had the absurd wish to close her eyes and hide.

'You will be able to find your way downstairs, *mademoiselle*?' he enquired slowly, his eyes moving back to her face.

'I'm sure I will.' Sarah spoke firmly but she felt her face begin to flush under the intent stare. She wanted him to go and she could not understand his reluctance to leave. He did not give the impression that he wanted to have any sort of conversation with her and the way he allowed his eyes to roam over her, summing her up, would, in any other circumstances, have annoyed Sarah immensely. But he was making her feel defenceless instead of angry and she couldn't think of one thing to say.

As he turned to leave there was suddenly a great clap of thunder and Sarah immediately stiffened up. Storms were not something she liked. She had been afraid of them since childhood and she looked anxiously at the window. It was now completely dark with the added and threatening darkness of a storm about to break fiercely.

Armand stopped, his eyes alert as he followed her gaze.

'You are afraid of storms?' he enquired softly and Sarah forced her eyes back to him.

'No, of course not.' She was not about to admit to any weakness but even as she said it her eyes were drawn reluctantly to the window again, where she was just in time to see an enormous flash of lightning. She bit into her lip worriedly and Armand strode across to draw the heavy curtains.

'You would not be placing yourself at a disadvantage to confess to a fear of storms,' he said with hard irritability. 'Even I am sometimes afraid of things.'

In spite of his unexpected act of kindness, Sarah wanted him out of her room fast and she was pleased when he went, closing the door firmly behind him. His eyes lingered on her until the last second, dark and impatient, and Sarah simply stared back, almost unable to move. Her skin was still hot, tingling, her eyes wide as they met his but his expression had not altered at all. It was just as unfathomable as when he had met her in Paris.

Sarah relaxed as he went. It was like being released from an invisible beam and she could not imagine anything that would make him afraid, ever. It would have to be ten feet tall and raging. She gave a little snort of annoyance as she took off her jacket. She was letting him worry her when normally she would have ignored anyone with his dubious courtesy.

There was a huge wardrobe and when she opened it there were plenty of coat hangers. This evening she would put her clothes away and then she would know for sure that she was staying for the whole month and fulfilling her father's wishes. It would be a sort of final step. It had meant a lot to him and she had promised readily to come, seeing the strain leave his face when she gave her word. He could have kept his secret, never told her about Céline, but she was glad now that he had told her. It seemed to bring him closer, being here with a woman he had loved for so long.

It did not take long to get ready for dinner because she had already decided what she would wear. She got out soft, dark green trousers and a long-sleeved tunic top that was heavily embroidered with flowers. It was sufficiently formal to meet the occasion that Céline was obviously planning but it was warm and comfortable and, after touching up her make-up and brushing her hair, Sarah was ready to go downstairs. She would be glad to get back into the cosiness of the kitchen because by now the storm was raging overhead, gathered around the château in full force, and, although she tried to ignore it, fear was too deeply rooted for her to succeed very well. She was thankful that she could not see the lightning.

She went out to the thickly carpeted passage and made her way quietly to the stairs and she was only a few steps down them when Armand came into the hall. He glanced up and saw her and seeing him gave her another jolt of surprise because he too had changed for dinner. He was dressed all in black—black trousers and open-necked shirt. Even though he wore no tie there was again this peculiar elegance about him that Sarah found increasingly fascinating. He was as dark as the storm and probably equally ferocious.

His eyes stayed on her with very frank appraisal and
Sarah tore her gaze away, walking down the stairs with
a rather shaky dignity. Her dignity was soon discarded,
however, as, without any sort of warning, the lights failed
and she was left in utter darkness except for the frequent
and blinding flashes of lightning that illuminated the hall
from the two round windows high up in the wall facing
her.

'Stay where you are!'

The sharp command kept her rooted to the spot. When
there was no flash of light it was impossible to see anything at all and she was well aware of the length and the
hardness of the stairs. She heard Armand coming up
towards her and with the next flash of lightning she found
his face very close to her own.

'I will see you safely down, *mademoiselle*,' he assured
her, taking her arm. 'If you should stumble, it is a long
way to fall.'

Sarah could only agree but she said nothing and even
with his hand on her arm in the blackness she only moved
hesitatingly forward, her feet searching for each step.
She had the uneasy feeling that if she fell she would pull
him down the stairs with her and she dared not even
think of how he would react to that.

Armand suddenly made a disgruntled sound deep in
his throat and Sarah was astonished and horrified to find
herself swept up into his arms. She could feel the strength
around her, as if she weighed nothing. Her own body
felt incredibly soft against the hard muscles and she
didn't know what to say. She had a tremendous desire
to struggle because her body reacted shockingly. The heat
flooded back into her skin, tingling and burning, almost
making her shudder. He held her with his arm beneath
her knees, his other arm across her back, his hand against
her ribs, just above her waist, and she felt a slow, hor-

rifying embarrassment as her breasts began to burgeon at the nearness of his hand.

Some slight sound of distress must have escaped from her because Armand gave a mutter of annoyance.

'You are perfectly safe,' he assured her impatiently. 'If we proceed at your pace, we may very well not reach the hall until morning.'

It was enough to silence her and she had too many problems at the moment to argue. Silence and stillness seemed to be of the utmost importance. When the next flash of lightning came, however, conflicting feelings battled and the old fear won. Sarah clutched at his shoulder, not caring what he made of that. He was strong, powerful, his arms like iron and the safest place at the moment was right where she was. What storm would dare strike at Armand Couvier?

'Safety comes in unexpected places, *mademoiselle*,' he murmured softly and, once again, she could almost hear the smile on his face and she knew it would be sardonic.

When they arrived in the hall, he put her firmly on her feet but kept a grip on her arm and Sarah was shakily pleased to see Céline appear, carrying a tall candle.

'Armand, what is happening? Why hasn't the emergency generator come on?'

'I have no idea. If you will take care of Mademoiselle Thorpe I will go and see to it.'

'Oh, not now, Armand,' Céline said fretfully. 'Do let it wait. Dinner is all ready and I am about to serve. We will eat by candlelight and you can look at the generator later.' She glanced over the flickering flame at Sarah and smiled. 'It is exciting, yes?'

'I do not think that Mademoiselle Thorpe finds it quite so exciting as you do,' Armand said drily. 'She is afraid of storms and the fact that the generator failed at a very inappropriate moment has made her wonder about her

safety in the château.' His hand left Sarah's arm and
the power stopped being transmitted from his fingertips
to her skin. 'Our English guest is nervous, Céline. We
will have to take good care of her.'

'Do not worry about the storm, *ma chère*,' Céline said
soothingly. 'They come and they go. You must surely
have storms in England.'

'Oh, yes.' Sarah managed a rather shaky laugh. 'I
don't like them any more there than I do here, however.'

'This is a French storm, *mademoiselle*,' Armand put
in sardonically. 'Much more terrifying. We are an
alarming race.' He politely indicated that they should
proceed to dinner and Sarah looked away from the eyes
that had now taken on an extra glitter from the flickering candle. He knew she was afraid but he didn't know
of her other, rather shameful problem. It was probably
tiredness or shock. She had nothing else to blame.

CHAPTER THREE

THE small dining-room was a sort of cosy little salon and again there was a huge original stone fireplace where a fire burned brightly, the light of the flames dancing about the room, adding to the flames of the candles that were already on the table. There was the same type of ornate, highly polished antique furniture and, in spite of its smallness, there was a certain amount of grandeur about the room.

To Sarah's surprise, Armand crossed to the window and closed the curtains. For a second his eyes met hers and although she waited for some sarcastic comment, some way he would find to ridicule her in front of his mother, he said absolutely nothing. He simply held her chair until she was seated and then performed the same service for his mother, which she was obviously quite used to. The food smelled delicious and, as Céline began to serve, Sarah knew that in spite of her nerves and her odd feelings she was going to eat everything that was placed before her.

If she had expected to be eating in an uncomfortable atmosphere she would have been wrong because Céline chatted away merrily, her eyes bright and interested on Sarah's face. The topic of conversation became books when Armand unexpectedly remarked that Sarah had a bookshop in England.

'Your father never told me that,' Céline said with an amused look on her face. 'I wonder why he did not? He was so proud of you, Sarah. I would have thought that he would also be proud that you are earning your own living.'

'So far I've spent more than I've earned,' Sarah confessed ruefully. 'It took a lot of money to set the shop up. It's in a good area so the rents are high. Many of the books were quite expensive to buy too, but I'm building up a clientele now and I'm rather pleased with the progress.'

Céline kept on the subject for a long time and Sarah was beginning to relax until Armand said rather abruptly, 'And how do you spend your leisure time, *mademoiselle*?'

Sarah instantly knew that something was wrong, although she did not know what it was, but she saw the sharp glance of annoyance that Céline threw towards Armand.

'There are plenty of theatres in London. I also swim, play tennis if the weather is good and of course I have friends. Besides, there was my father.' Her voice fell and Céline intervened.

'You were very close, were you not?' she asked softly and Sarah was only too ready to agree. She didn't keep the subject up because she felt rather lost, no longer interested in conversation. Things had happened too quickly, things that had swept her along. She still had not had time to mourn and her final act had been to quarrel with Craig who quite unexpectedly seemed to be the only one she had left to confide in. Sadness swept over her and she was silent.

Her father's death had left a huge gap in her life. It was true that she had many friends but none of them was close. Craig was now closer to her than anyone but, even so, she was uncomfortable and uneasy with his business acquaintances. She could not settle with any ease into his way of life, the clubs he owned and frequented, the deals he seemed to be constantly making with people who worried her.

Craig expected her to make an effort with them and although she had tried it was impossible sometimes. It led to friction and it had been this constant backing away from his life that had driven Craig to annoyance when she had left for France. In many ways she could not blame him but he made her feel trapped now that her father was no longer there.

With an understanding that Sarah would not have expected, Céline turned to Armand and began to talk about the land. They still spoke in English but it was all about farming, the fields, the men, the animals, Armand's plans for tomorrow and how this storm would affect things. Sarah was grateful and was quite happy to eat in silence.

Later she offered to help with the dishes and Céline was almost shocked.

'The château is old, *ma chère*, but, as you have seen from the appliances in the kitchen, we do not entirely live in the past. There is a dishwasher which will adequately take care of these—if we have electricity.'

She began to load them skilfully on to a trolley and would not hear of Sarah helping.

They were drinking coffee when the lights came on and Céline looked with amusement at the signs of gratitude on Sarah's face.

'You see?' she said comfortably. 'Things sort themselves out.'

'And things behave in mysterious ways,' Armand murmured sardonically, rising from the table. 'I will check out the emergency generator. I would not like Mademoiselle Thorpe to awake in the night and find herself in alarming darkness.'

He left the room and Sarah felt herself relax at once. It was only then that she realised what a state of tension she had been in merely because he was sitting at the same table. She hoped he would be very busy during the time she was to spend here, otherwise she would be screaming with nerves and irritation before long.

She trailed into the kitchen behind Céline, taking her coffee with her and watching as Céline dealt swiftly with the dishes.

'You will get used to Armand,' Céline said quietly. 'He is not quite as ferocious as he appears to be.'

'I expect he'll be very busy and I won't see much of him,' Sarah said hopefully and Céline's next words really stunned her.

'He is very much pressed for time at the moment and this storm is not to his liking. It will hold things up. Armand is only here for another two weeks.'

'He is going away, *madame*?'

'Oh, Armand does not live here! This is *my* house. It has never belonged to the Couviers. It was left to me by my father. Of course, one day it will be Armand's to add to his inheritance but for now it is mine. Armand lives in Paris,' she continued as Sarah listened in amazement. 'From time to time during each year he comes back and manages this place, makes sure that everything is as it should be and that the men are doing their work. He has been here for a week already and he can, perhaps, spare another two weeks although it may be even less, but after that he goes back.'

'He—he works in Paris, *madame*?'

'But of course, Sarah! Did he not tell you?' Céline looked exasperated but then she shrugged. 'It is only what I would have expected. When Armand feels that it is not necessary to say something, he does not say it. I had better tell you myself.' She leaned against the table and contemplated the glowing fire. 'My husband left Armand with a very large business to run. The Couvier wealth originally started in paper mills. They made very exclusive paper; in fact, they still do but that was a couple of generations ago, of course.

'Now things have grown. My husband and his father before him were very astute businessmen, as is Armand. Many things were added. There are now business interests all over France and in several European countries. You might say that Armand sits at the head of a business empire. It takes up all his time and it is only because, like me, he has a love of the land that he comes back to this place. His strength and the love of the rather wild landscape he inherited from me and I know that when anything happens to me he will never let this château go. He has his father's business acumen, however, and although he works all hours he enjoys it.'

She gave an amused little sigh and switched on the machine.

'And now, *ma chère*, you look very tired. I will take you to your room, just in case the lights go out again, although I very much doubt it. Armand is seeing to the generator and surely it would not dare to fail him?'

Sarah was pleased to go before he came back and she could not imagine any mere machine defying Armand. Céline had confirmed her already growing suspicions that Armand was a very complex character. He would be if he was head of a huge business and then suddenly a man who worked on the land. It didn't make her understand him any more—in fact she understood him even less—but she was beginning to see why he had this air of elegance that sat so strangely with his stormy, brooding good looks.

She was glad he would be returning to Paris. It would give her the chance to spend the promised month here without any complications and she was well aware that plenty of complications could arise when a man so disturbing as Armand Couvier was around.

*   *   *

To her surprise, Sarah slept deeply. The room was warm, the bed comfortable and, for now at least, the storm had passed. She went so far as to draw the curtains back and saw that there was a fitful moon, clouds scudding across it. Tonight she had promised to ring Craig, to tell him she had arrived safely but, in the upheaval brought by the storm and with her uneasy awareness of Armand, she had forgotten.

In any case she was still smarting from her final words with Craig and at the moment she felt she could not cope with more trouble. The quarrel had merely added to the stress she was under and she thought with some surprise that it was odd that the hostility and pressure she had felt coming from Armand had not left her with any feeling of more stress.

It was true that he alarmed her but he was so much outside her understanding that there was a reluctant feeling of fascination there, too. She went to sleep with the thought of that stormy face, those dark and intent eyes in her mind. He was very much like the land, part of the ambience of this place, and she found it hard to imagine him living in Paris and wielding power as the head of a huge business.

Power came easily to him, but not patience, she suspected. To work for him must be a nightmare and for a moment she fantasised about being his secretary and opening the door to his office to find the hostile eyes aimed at her like a weapon. She knew she would scurry away, back to safety, and with that her mind returned to England, her small but pleasant shop and her ordered way of life. She would ring Craig tomorrow because if he made her uneasy it was certainly not the sort of uneasiness she felt with Armand.

Sarah awoke the next morning to find cold sunlight streaming into the room and for a few moments she was rather surprised to find that she had left the curtains open all night. She must be braver than she imagined and, if the storm had come back she certainly hadn't heard it. She was still warm and comfortable in the bed and didn't really want to get up but she knew she must make an effort.

The sound of voices outside had her getting out of bed quickly to walk to the window. When she looked down, she could see a Land Rover parked beside Armand's car where he had left it the night before. The whole morning seemed to be glittering with light, the leaves and the grass still wet from the night's storm. There was a fresh, bright look about everything and the gloom and menace of the previous evening had gone completely.

From her window she could see a long way and the spire of a church proclaimed that a village was not too far off. The thought brightened Sarah up. When she could, she would go to the village and have a look around. French village shops fascinated her. They always seemed to be much more sophisticated than their English counterparts. Even in small villages it was possible to buy smart and unexpected things.

As she stood there, Armand walked towards the Land Rover. He was accompanied by two men and they were all talking animatedly. No doubt they were planning the day's activities and Sarah watched, her eyes drawn to him in fascination, even though she found him so irritating.

He stood much taller than the other men, the same power about him that she had seen the night before and, watching him secretly from here, she felt an almost guilty flood of attraction. There was a magnetism about him that merely increased every time she saw him. It was safe to have feelings from this distance but she knew that once he either looked at her or spoke her defence mechanism would go into action and she would feel only alarm.

He was wearing jeans and sweater, high boots and a dark, thickly padded jacket. In spite of the obvious cold of the day, his head was uncovered and once again she saw that thick dark hair blown by the wind. Even if they had been close enough for her to hear their actual conversation she could not have understood them because the French was very rapid and her own French was quite halting, although she understood most things that were said to her in that language.

After a minute, the men nodded and went in opposite directions and Armand opened the door of the Land Rover to climb inside. She was intent on watching him to the last second and she pressed closer to the window. As she did so, Armand slowly glanced up and Sarah saw a wry smile touch his lips and grow until his face was softened with amusement. It was only then that she realised he could see her clearly. She was standing there in full view, wearing nothing but her lace-topped nightdress.

She very quickly moved out of sight, greatly relieved to hear the sound of the Land Rover pulling away. Not a very good beginning to the morning! It looked as if every time she saw Armand things were going to go wrong. What would he be thinking now? It almost looked as if she had done it deliberately and she hadn't the slightest doubt that he would draw the worst possible conclusions. She hoped he would not come in for lunch but she strongly suspected that he would.

Sarah made her way down to the bright kitchen to have breakfast with Céline and she was introduced to the two women who had arrived to clean the rooms. One of them went off immediately to start work but the other one, Mathilde, stood around, tidying the kitchen and chatting to Céline, her bright eyes lingering with interest on Sarah's astonishingly fair hair.

After breakfast, Sarah went to her room to set about the task she had intended to undertake the night before—putting her clothes into the large wardrobe. It occupied her for some time and later she went to stand by the window and look out over the parkland that surrounded the château. She could see no sign of activity either there or in the fields close by and she felt a little more safe with Armand out of sight. Her mind went to the village as her eyes once again fell on the church. She wondered if Céline had a car that she could borrow one day so that she could go there, or maybe she could go with Céline? It would be a good way of getting to know her.

She felt much more cheerful this morning and just as she was leaving the room Mathilde knocked and came in. For a little while, Sarah spoke to her in her rather halting French, inordinately pleased with herself that she was readily understood but utterly confounded when Mathilde then spoke to her in English. It must have been her way of showing give and take, and Sarah was astounded.

The woman was handsome-looking, rosy-cheeked and plump, and when Sarah went down to the kitchen to find Céline she remarked on this fact and told her about the mutual language lessons, to Céline's obvious amusement.

'She is showing her approval,' she assured Sarah. 'Mathilde thinks you are the most beautiful thing she has ever seen—so fair, so slender, with eyes like a young fawn. As to her own figure and the rosy cheeks, it is because she is from good, healthy stock! That is what we are in these parts, Sarah. To all intents and purposes, Armand is a Parisian but he gets his tremendous physical strength from this land and from *my* people.'

Sarah could believe it but she did not wish to be reminded of Armand. Looking down from the window at him, she had already seen more of him than she wished to see. He had also seen a little too much of her. She pushed him very hastily from her mind where he seemed to be lingering far too much.

Céline was swift and businesslike in all her movements and Sarah did not like to intrude. She therefore felt quite at a loss as to what to do.

'Don't feel that you must be near me all the time, *ma chère*,' Céline said comfortably. 'There are four good weeks and we will get to know each other slowly and carefully, yes? In the meantime, if there is anything you wish to do it is perfectly all right.' She smiled across at Sarah. 'Why not put on your coat and have a look around the château? It is cold by the look of it but at least there is no rain at the moment.'

'Oh, I really would like to do that,' Sarah said enthusiastically and Céline told her that there was a courtyard round the back where most of the farm buildings were.

'This is not one of the really splendid châteaux that you will find along the Loire,' she admitted. 'It has always been a place for working. We farm the land and watch things grow. It is not much changed in all the years.'

Another glance at the bright sky made Sarah determined to get out and explore and she went back upstairs to get a coat. She was already wearing thick corduroy trousers and a deep blue sweater this morning and she found a light but warm jacket she had put into the wardrobe. She had only packed warm things to come here and it looked as if she would need them.

She went down and let herself out of the front door, breathing in the fresh, crisp air. As Armand had said, this was not really the time of the year to visit the north

of France but there was an unusual attractiveness about
it.

Sarah looked across the parkland where tall, sturdy
trees grew that were perhaps even older than the château
itself. Later she would walk among them but at the
moment she was more interested in exploring the outside
of the château and she decided to take Céline's advice
and go round to the courtyard.

She could see as she walked along that when spring
was really upon them the front of the château would be
surrounded by flowers. Everything was well cared for
and new grass was just springing up on the wide lawns.
At one side was a little stream that even now was gurgling
along coldly. This would be a wonderful place in summer
and already she could see why it meant so much to Céline
in addition to the fact that it was her family home.

The entrance to the courtyard was marked by a little
door set into the great stone walls and Sarah wondered
how tractors and other farm machinery could gain entrance but as she stepped through the gate she could see
that if she had come the other way there was a wide
opening.

The courtyard was huge and cobbled, with buildings
all around it, some of the doors open, and Sarah felt a
flurry of alarm when she saw the Land Rover that
Armand had left in earlier parked to one side. She expected to see him instantly and almost fled right then
but there was no sound anywhere and she remembered
that while she had been having breakfast she had heard
the noise of some vehicle and, later, the noise of a tractor.
She decided that he had probably brought the Land
Rover back and taken the tractor out. It eased her mind
and she relaxed from her wary stance and began to
explore.

When she looked up at the château from the back, it
seemed to be even more towering, with a permanence

about it that was oddly reassuring. There must be many rooms that she had not seen, rooms reached by some staircase, probably one that led off from one of the upstairs passages. She stepped back to look at the smaller windows so high up. In older days, the rooms there had probably been for servants but she could not imagine Mathilde taking kindly to being housed so high up, sturdy though she was.

With her rather romantic mind spinning back to days long past and peopling the château with ladies who arrived in horse-drawn carriages, Sarah walked across to the buildings. Céline would look good in long, extravagant dresses but she felt quite a stirring of vexation when Armand refused to fit into her dreams. He would not fade into her imagined scenario. He was much too real, much too immediate.

To her great joy, one of the buildings contained two horses, comfortably stabled. She spent a few minutes talking to them, fondling their velvet noses, and was happy to realise that a sort of peace was beginning to descend upon her, a feeling she had never expected to find here. Was this what her father had wanted? Had he known that this place would help her to recover from her loss?

He had always given her so much love that she had been speaking only the truth when she had told Céline that she bore no resentment. Love was an emotion that grew with sharing and she had the feeling that Céline would have agreed with her. There was enormous understanding in those dark eyes. They were very different from Armand's dark eyes. Somehow she felt that he would look upon love with sardonic amusement. She could never imagine the time, past or present, when he would have needed love.

She had just walked into the largest building, which was obviously some sort of barn, when she heard a sound above her. She had felt so calm, so alone, and the noise startled her. Looking up, she saw Armand standing there, simply watching her, and she almost turned and ran out right then because her heart began to thump alarmingly. It was obvious that he had heard her footsteps and waited to see who it was. Now he knew and she had no choice but to stay or run and look idiotic.

There was a flight of wooden steps that led to what was quite obviously the hay-loft. Plenty of it was stored up there and Armand had a rake in his hand, his towering presence made even more so by the height of the building.

'*Bonjour, mademoiselle.*' There was still a look of wry amusement about him and Sarah suspected that he was remembering his sight of her this morning. Even his voice was softly amused and to her annoyance she felt her face begin to burn.

'*Bonjour, monsieur.*' The dark eyebrows rose in surprise at her firm reply. 'You speak French, *mademoiselle*? Or is this just a polite repetition of my greeting?'

'I do speak French, but very little and not very often,' Sarah confessed hastily, worried that he would suddenly speak in that rapid way she had heard this morning and still slightly unnerved by Mathilde's little demonstration of linguistic skills. 'I can understand French very well indeed but I'm a bit too scared to speak it.'

'Scared?' He dropped the rake into the hay and came slowly down the steps, still watching her curiously. 'Ah! You mean that you are afraid!'

'Nervous,' she corrected, folding her hands in front of her with a definite air of nervousness right at that moment. 'You see, I always know what I'm going to say but when I'm faced with actually saying it—I panic.'

For the first time ever, she saw him grin, the flash of white teeth against his dark face, the low sound of laughter in the back of his throat.

'You are much given to nerves, I fear, *mademoiselle*,' he pointed out drily. 'Last night, the storm, this morning, the language. I rather think you were also overwhelmed by nerves when I picked you up in Paris.'

Sarah cast a reproachful look at him, her soft mouth tightening primly.

'You did nothing to ease my nerves, *monsieur*,' she assured him with reproof in her voice. 'You must have known that I was anxious and yet you made me more anxious still.'

'Did I?' he asked wryly. 'You must forgive me, *mademoiselle*. I have a very bad temper and I did not particularly wish to come to Paris. I see too much of Paris to go there willingly when I need not. As I was extremely busy and this concerned only my mother and yourself, I regret to say that I was rather irritated at being a taxi driver. If I alarmed you, I apologise.'

Sarah cast a quick look at him and then hastily looked away. She wished she had not come right into this building. It was rather dim, atmospheric, pushing her mind back into the château's past. She could see the sunny courtyard outside and wished herself back in it, with Armand a great distance from her. Her imagination was a little too strong to be comfortable in this old building with this overwhelming man.

He was now standing at the bottom of the steps, watching her, with that same assessing look in his eyes she had seen before. He was probably trying to work out how she could be so scared, stupid and ineffectual and Sarah snapped out of her uneasy contemplation of him.

'I—I'll let you get on about your affairs, *monsieur*,' she managed quite firmly. 'I know how busy you are; your mother told me.'

'Ah! Céline has been acquainting you with all the facts? It is only what I could have expected.'

'I was just surprised that you were leaving so soon,' Sarah said quickly, wondering if Armand ever quarrelled with his mother, and certainly wanting to keep Céline out of trouble. She didn't add that she had been very relieved to hear that he would soon be gone but from the look on his face she suspected that he knew.

'Call me, Armand,' he suggested softly. 'Perhaps with a little practice we will manage to be almost civil with each other?'

Sarah looked very doubtful at that and once again she saw him smile. It was merely a flash of amusement and she was very pleased when he began to make his way to the door. She followed quickly, no longer wanting to be in this darkened building, and he glanced round at her as she rather hurriedly stepped into the sunlight.

'You are having an attack of nerves again? You are now afraid of dim light, *mademoiselle*?' he asked.

Sarah's lips tightened in annoyance. He had invited her to call him Armand but obviously she could not because he clearly had every intention of continuing to call her *mademoiselle*. He was much too astute, in any case, even picking up her anxious vibes. Her mind would soon not be her own at all.

'I'm not afraid, *monsieur*,' she said sharply. 'Your mother suggested that I look around the château. That barn was just one of the places I looked in and now I've seen it!'

'Then look in all the other places,' he advised, back to derision, one dark brow raised sceptically, 'but I assure you, *mademoiselle*, that there is nothing spectacular, exciting nor alarming in any of the buildings.'

Sarah silently begged to differ. There had been something spectacular, exciting and alarming when she had entered that particular building: Armand himself. Her face felt hot as this thought came unwarily into her mind.

'Are you going back to the fields?' she asked hopefully and he glanced at her quickly.

'You wish to be rid of me? Yes, I am going; fear not.' They were in the middle of the courtyard now, much to Sarah's relief, and he suddenly turned to her. 'What are you going to do with your time while you are here?' he asked. 'You will soon become bored with farm buildings.'

'I'm going to get to know your mother as my father wished. I'm going to walk if the weather is good and I intend to go to the village I can see from my bedroom window.'

Armand gave a long, slow smile, his eyes slanting over her.

'Ah, yes! Your bedroom window...'

For a moment his eyes held hers and Sarah felt the colour running hotly under her skin. That had been a stupid thing to say and he had picked up on it immediately. She really would have to watch her words.

He went across to the Land Rover and Sarah found herself following him, much to her annoyance. She stopped and stood quite still when she realised what she was doing. He got inside and, while the door was still open, he looked across at her.

'Any time you wish to go to the village I will take you,' he offered blandly. 'I would not want you to feel isolated here. Before very long you will be missing your life in London and then you will flee and forget this promise.'

'I will not forget my promise, *monsieur*!' Sarah said starchily, her hands clenched at her side in annoyance, and he grinned at her again just before he closed the door.

'Call me Armand,' he urged softly. '*A bientôt*, Sarah.'

He started the engine and the heavy vehicle swept out of the yard, handled with the same skill he used when he was driving his car, and Sarah stared after him, frowning madly. How infuriating he was! He had actually called her by her name but somehow it had been like a challenge. She shook herself out of the stupor that seemed to be gripping her and strode out of the courtyard, determined now to explore the parkland, and she was irritated to find that, as the Land Rover left, a good deal of the excitement seemed to have gone out of the morning.

If she started to let her thoughts dwell on things like that, she would certainly not be able to stay here for four weeks and keep her promise. But then, Armand would not be here for much longer. Two weeks at the most, Céline had said. Sarah hoped he would leave before that; he was having far too much of an effect on her already.

He did not come in for his lunch and although Sarah did not remark on the fact Céline said that sometimes, if Armand was very busy, he came in late, had his lunch quickly and then left again.

'He is never still while he is here and sometimes I feel guilty about it,' she confessed, 'but it is his own idea. I really think that the few weeks he spends here keep him sane in the turmoil of Paris. He is cool and level-headed by nature but I think his time here tops him up. I would imagine that when he goes back afterwards people feel the sharp edge of his tongue.'

She laughed quietly and Sarah could see that Céline was proud of the sharp edge of Armand's tongue. There was a good deal about them that was alike and Sarah could not quite understand why she felt so comfortable with this woman and yet so uncomfortable with her son.

After lunch, at Céline's invitation, Sarah explored the château and was delighted to find that although many of the rooms were not in use, they were all in the same beautiful condition as the rooms below. She went to the very high rooms last of all and from there she had her first glimpse of the sea. As she moved to another window she could see the village again but from here the view was much better. From this height it appeared to be quite close, down several winding lanes from the château, and Sarah stood staring at it for a while.

It looked absolutely delightful. Intriguing streets meandered between timbered buildings, with a church standing just off the square, tall trees that looked like chestnuts surrounding it. She could see the red and white striped awning of some café or restaurant and Sarah was suddenly impatient to go to the village and explore.

CHAPTER FOUR

SARAH felt a quick charge of energy that yesterday she had imagined would never come back and as it was still light and only early afternoon she put on her jacket and told Céline that she was going for a walk. She slipped her purse into her pocket and decided that, after all the trouble she had been through during the past few weeks, a very brisk walk would do her good.

She had noticed a path that led across the fields and she knew that if she went that way she would not have to go down the long, twisting drive. It would save a lot of time and her feelings were almost gleeful as she set off. The sun cheered her up and she loved walking. It would be rather awkward if she encountered Armand after his offer to take her to the village but she would just have to brazen it out if he appeared.

Partway down the drive she climbed a stile and crossed the field towards the side nearest to the village, smiling to herself that this small thing was almost like an adventure. The wind was blowing very strongly and she pulled her long hair over her shoulder, clasping it with her hand, realising that she would have been well-advised to wear a cap. She was not made of the sturdy stuff that Armand was and it was much more chilly out here than she had imagined. Nothing would have made her go back, however, and she turned up her collar and strode on, her mind set on the little village and the interesting shops she was sure would be there.

As she came to the end of the field, Sarah found that there was no stile here and she had to climb the fence to get into the road. It was rather difficult and she was just on top of it, balanced precariously, when the Land Rover came past and stopped, Armand getting out to stare at her in surprise.

'You are running away so soon?' he asked. He stood with his hands flat on the bonnet and regarded her with sardonic amusement.

Perched on top of the fence, Sarah felt slightly ridiculous and quite guilty about her sneaky trip when he had offered to take her but she stayed where she was. It put distance between them and that could only be good.

'I was going for a walk,' she said calmly, sitting on the top bar of the fence and smiling a little tightly. 'I thought I might even make it to the village.'

The dark eyebrows rose inquiringly.

'You did not like my offer to escort you? I am disappointed. However, the village is much further away than it appears to be from the château. If you had arrived there, I fear you would not have been back before dark. What would you have done then, *mademoiselle*, especially if the storm returns?'

Sarah hadn't thought of that at all and she looked quickly around. The sky was coldly blue with the sun still shining and she knew he was just goading her.

'There's no sign of a storm,' she said quite crossly.

'You will have observed, perhaps, that we are quite close to the sea and you know as well as I do that storms roll up very quickly, quite often at this time of the year. In any case, consider how your nerves would react to a walk back to the château in the dark.'

It quite worried Sarah and her face fell, gloom descending at the idea that she would have to give up her plans and retreat ignominiously. She felt almost mutinous about things and she heard Armand give a low chuckle of amusement before he strode round the bonnet of the Land Rover and came towards her.

'You look like a rebellious child who has been cautioned about her conduct,' he said quietly, walking to the fence and looking up at her. 'I feel like a villain. Your mind must really be very set upon this expedition. *Alors*! I will take you.'

He reached up, his strong hands coming round her waist and Sarah had no time to feel alarm before he had lifted her down and released her.

'Come!' he urged when she simply stood and stared up at him. 'I will take you to the village.'

'But you haven't got the time!' Now she felt very guilty and also she had intended to go alone, not to place herself close to a man she wished to avoid for a variety of reasons.

'For you, I will make the time,' he murmured silkily. 'Céline prizes you highly. You are, after all, John Thorpe's daughter.'

'Don't imagine you can embarrass me with remarks like that,' Sarah said crossly, planting her feet firmly and looking up at him with stormy eyes, her hair held tightly by her hand because of the brisk wind. 'I meant what I said to your mother. She gave my father happiness and that's the best gift you can give anyone. I approve of their relationship, whatever *you* think of it.'

'You imagine that I disapprove?' He was standing with his back to the wind, his powerful body sheltering her, and Sarah felt very small at his side. From amusement to quiet darkness, he had once again moved into the ambience of the land. 'I heard at least part of what you said to Céline. You remember your mother? I also remember. I remember my father and I remember well. To my mind she should have left him and lived openly with her lover. They would have then had more time together, more sweet memories and you would not now be here getting to know her so belatedly. They should have married, no matter what the consequences.'

The thick hair was once again blown across his forehead and the dark eyes held hers imperiously. Sarah felt that he could have stood there through a storm, unmoving, implacable. She had never before met such a forceful man, never seen anyone with such potent masculinity. Even when he said nothing, his presence was commanding and there was a leashed-in energy about him that almost made her breathless.

'Initially your father was alive,' she said quietly, tearing her eyes away from their fascinated appraisal of him. 'Later I think they were just—just comfortable as they were.'

'Comfortable?' he queried scornfully. 'Perhaps. However, I find it astonishing to believe. I cannot doubt that they loved each other but I would not be content to live as they lived for any reason whatever. To love a woman and not wish to hold her in my arms all night and every night is beyond my understanding.'

A peculiar shiver ran over Sarah's skin that was nothing to do with the sharp wind. Once again, her imagination took hold of her and she felt her heart accelerate at the thought of Armand's strong arms around the woman he loved, holding her in the night. A picture of herself came into her head and, terrified, she thrust it away with speed. She was quite mad!

'People are different,' she said primly, 'which is just as well. It wouldn't do for everyone to be alike.'

Armand began to laugh quietly and his brown hand tilted her chin.

'I detect the prudish English mind,' he said in an amused voice. 'Which is quite odd—in the circumstances.'

'What circumstances?' Sarah demanded, ready to pick a fight rather than allow her mind to wander along dangerous paths.

'Your approval of their liaison,' he said drily. 'How can you approve of your father having a mistress for twenty years and then speak in that strait-laced manner as if you detected something quite unspeakable? If they had followed their hearts' desire and lived openly together, you and I would have been the very best of friends by now. Imagine that.'

'I have a very poor imagination,' Sarah lied stiffly and Armand smiled even more broadly.

'Then why are you afraid of storms, dark buildings and me?' he enquired softly.

'Sheer common sense! And—and in any case I'm not afraid of you,' she added hastily.

He shot a look of deep irony at her as he took her arm and led her to the Land Rover whether she wanted to go with him or not.

'I had not intended to stand chatting with you,' he pointed out slightly impatiently as he climbed in beside her and started the engine. 'I can see that you will waste a good deal of my valuable time if I am not extremely careful.'

'I didn't ask you to take me anywhere!' Sarah snapped. 'Just let me out and I'll walk!'

'Certainly not. I would only have to come and search for you when you found yourself overtaken by night on the way back,' he murmured sardonically. 'It is easier to act as your chauffeur. I will know exactly where you are, without the task of looking under every bush in the darkness to find your hiding place.'

Sarah glared at him but he ignored her and the vehicle roared away down the road to the village. Secretly, she was glad to be inside and out of the wind. Her ears were ringing with the cold and she had the uneasy feeling that her nose was red. Even if she hadn't been glad, it was obvious that Armand would not stop at all. For reasons known only to himself, he had decided to take her to the village. Well, it didn't matter; she would just have to watch her words and her imagination.

When they arrived, Sarah was pleased to find that it was exactly as she had thought and she was eager to look at everything and find her way to the shops, a satisfied expression on her face that attracted Armand's sardonic attention at once.

'You look exactly like a woman who has scented shopping,' he remarked with an interested glance at her. 'We will have coffee. You are cold.'

'I'll warm up quickly,' Sarah assured him, anxious to be off on her explorations and leave him behind.

'You will warm up more quickly with a hot coffee inside you,' he countered firmly. 'If you catch a chill, Céline will look for someone to blame. It will be me, I suspect. Do not imagine either that I will allow you to move out of my sight. I do not intend to spend the evening searching for you.'

'How could I get lost in this small place?' Sarah asked impatiently, glaring up at him, and he looked at her wryly.

'How indeed? I am sure you would discover a way.'

'I'm not an incompetent idiot!' Sarah pointed out crossly but he took her arm, leading her firmly to a nearby café.

'Really? You surprise me,' he murmured mockingly.

She decided that in spite of her growing fascination he was infuriating, even when she found herself in blissful warmth and smelled the aroma of good, French coffee. He would always think he knew best. The fact that he probably did was neither here nor there. At the moment she had her mind set on the shops and she had no desire to sit facing Armand; in fact she was quite anxious not to face him at all.

He was greeted with obvious pleasure by all the people there and Sarah sighed with resignation. It looked as if her shopping expedition would have to wait, unless she made a quick lunge for the door and ran off. She gave a longing look at the outside but Armand took her arm, leading her to a seat, and when she looked up glumly he was grinning at her.

'There would be little point in making a run for the shops, *mademoiselle*,' he assured her wryly. 'Today is the day they close for the afternoon. It is what you call in England the half-day closing.'

'Why, you...!' Sarah stared at him in outrage. 'You knew all the time and yet you dragged me here...'

'I did not drag you,' he complained in a taunting voice. 'You came in comfort. How could I leave you hovering on the fence? You needed to be rescued and I owe a duty to my mother. If I see you in trouble I will get you out of it, *n'est-ce pas*?'

Sarah subsided into tight-lipped silence. Her expedition was a flop and he had known that from the moment he had seen her. He was simply amusing himself at her expense.

'You could have just told me about the shops and let me go back to the château. Anyway, I thought you were extremely busy?' she said crossly and Armand gave a very Gallic shrug.

'I needed some light entertainment. Your peculiar ways are beginning to be very entertaining, *mademoiselle*.'

'My ways are not peculiar and I am not at all entertaining!' Sarah snapped and he gave her a long, ironic glance.

'But of course you are. Did you not start my day with light entertainment?'

He didn't have to say any more. Sarah knew what he meant and her face flooded with colour when she remembered standing at the bedroom window and gazing down at him. She couldn't think of anything at all to say. She just looked helplessly into her coffee, wishing the floor would open and swallow her up.

'I'm sorry,' Armand said after a second. 'Things like that do not amuse you, do they? Céline suspects that I am a brute. She is probably right. For a moment I forgot that you are English and still very young.'

Sarah looked up, astonished at the apology, and found him smiling at her quite ruefully.

'I'm twenty-three,' she managed quietly. 'That's not very young.'

'And I am thirty-four. Old enough to know better than to tease in that manner.'

'It's all right,' Sarah muttered. 'I don't mind.'

'You do,' he pointed out softly. 'In future I will watch the step.'

'Your step,' Sarah corrected absently and he grinned at her.

'Did I not say so?'

She shook her head in exasperation as she realised he was deliberately adjusting his excellent and fluent English to tease her further. Still, he had apologised but it had left her feeling rather foolish, perhaps even childish. The women Craig knew would have laughed, or even flirted. Probably the women Armand knew would have done the same. All she had been able to do was attempt to hide in silence.

In spite of her embarrassment, Sarah soon began to relax and look around the bright little café and the people who were there. Plenty of them came across to speak to Armand but the words were swift and quite beyond her. Armand never bothered to introduce her until an older man came in. He was tall, well-dressed and his face lit up when he saw them.

'Armand! It is not usual to find you here at this time of the day.' He came straight across and Armand smiled up at him.

'I brought Mademoiselle Thorpe for a coffee,' he said in English. 'She is staying with my mother. She is—a friend from England.'

'I am pleased to meet you, *mademoiselle*,' the man said while Sarah was observing how Armand had rather skilfully explained her presence and her relationship to his mother. 'I am Eric De Brise and, as Armand will tell you if I do not mention it myself, I am the local doctor.'

He ordered a coffee and Armand invited him to join them at their table.

'I don't suppose you will be in here for very long, rushing about as you usually do?'

'No. I spared a little time to entertain Mademoiselle Thorpe but when we have finished our coffee we must go back. I still have things to do.'

'Violette is coming home,' Eric De Brise suddenly said with a quick glance at Armand.

'I know. She phoned me last week.'

'I might have known I would be the last to be informed.' De Brise smiled. 'Six months. It has been a long time, *n'est-ce-pas*, *mon ami*?'

'A very long time,' Armand agreed and Eric De Brise began to laugh.

'*Mais oui!*' he observed with an amused look at Armand's impassive face. 'A long, hard winter.' He turned to Sarah. 'Violette is my daughter, *mademoiselle*. She works in advertising and for the last six months she has been working in Italy. Fortunately for all of us she is now coming back. Normally she works in Paris and I suspect that that is because Armand is there.'

Sarah hoped she was smiling in all the right places. She didn't really know what to say and Armand looked extremely disgruntled that his private affairs were being discussed in front of her. Of course, it wasn't surprising that he had some woman in his life. He was a very attractive and unusual man and Sarah mused that in spite of Céline's explanations she knew almost nothing of Armand.

On the way back to the château he was very silent, nothing left of the rather teasing person he had become earlier. As they were going up the drive, Sarah pulled herself out of her own quite gloomy silence.

'Thank you for taking me,' she said, forcing brightness into her voice. 'It was very kind of you, even if I didn't get to the shops.'

'I am not kind, *mademoiselle*,' he said with the harshness that had disappeared earlier. 'Surely you realise that? I rescued you from a situation, just as I brought you from the airport. As my mother will no doubt tell you, kindness and I do not sit easily together.'

'I can well believe it!' Sarah assured him sharply, stung by his hard reply to her polite thanks. 'However, as it doesn't concern me, I can afford to ignore it.'

'So you bite back when bitten, *mademoiselle*?' he mused quietly. 'I was beginning to imagine that you were merely a delicate English flower with little substance.'

'The English rose has sharp thorns, *monsieur*!' Sarah said angrily. 'I would have thought you would know that.'

'I am learning,' he murmured. There was a look of amusement on his face again but this time Sarah was extremely disgruntled herself. Mulling it over, she decided that he had quite spoiled her day. He had embarrassed her this morning, appeared in the barn when she had not expected him and then he had deliberately taken her to closed shops. If he was annoyed that Dr De Brise had spoken about things he wished to remain private, he shouldn't have taken her with him.

He dropped her at the front steps before driving round to the courtyard at the back and Sarah didn't even look at him. She deliberately refused to say thank you and was glad to get into the warmth of the kitchen; at least

Céline was smiling and extremely normal. If Armand thought it was unusual to be somebody's mistress for so long then he should take a good look at himself. It was better to be very unusual than unusual *and* grimly bad-tempered.

'You came back with Armand!' Céline exclaimed in surprise. 'Did he find you on your walk?'

'He took me into the village for a coffee. It was very interesting. I had hoped to go to the shops but they were closed.'

'Ah, yes. They close today in the afternoon but it is the only time, except for Sunday, of course. I will be going. You can go with me.'

'That would be nice.' Sarah was relieved to know that she would be able to go out with Céline. She did not intend to place herself in any uncomfortable situation with Armand in future and she certainly wanted to see more of Céline.

'Well, did you like our little café?' asked Céline as she bustled about the kitchen making tea.

'Yes. Armand seemed to know everyone.'

'But of course, *ma chère*. Armand was here for many years of his life—until his father got his claws into him,' she added in a bitter voice. 'To my mind he is still more happy here than in Paris but he would never leave the business, of course; he needs the excitement of it, even if the business could manage without him, which it cannot.'

She sat at the table and poured tea that Sarah didn't really want. She was feeling gloomy after the trip to the village. Any brightness she had felt earlier seemed to have gone and it was not her fault that Dr De Brise had talked about Armand and Violette.

'I met Dr De Brise,' she told Céline, hoping to get more information and disgusted with herself for bothering. A quirk of amusement came to Céline's face.

'I suppose he was proudly telling you about Violette?' she asked wryly.

'Yes. He said she was coming home from Italy.'

'Oh, I can imagine. He is extremely proud of that, too. Of course, Violette has known Armand since they were children. She is close to his age and she is more of a match for Armand. Like him, she is strong, though sometimes, I think, a little too possessive. Even as a child she was like that but then I suppose that anyone with a gentle nature would be overwhelmed by Armand's character. Sometimes he is quite alarming. Do you not think so?'

'Sometimes,' Sarah agreed. In fact she had no idea what to say. She was very annoyed with herself. Why she should be worried and upset about someone who was obviously Armand's long-standing girlfriend she did not know. How Armand Couvier conducted his life was none of her affair.

She remembered that she had not yet phoned Craig and now was a very good time to do it, while she was in this grumpy mood. It might just cheer her up and if he was annoyed she would be more forceful.

'Do you think, *madame*, that I could possibly phone England?' she asked. 'I promised to phone but I forgot, in all the excitement of coming here.'

'In all the turmoil of coming here, Sarah,' Céline corrected her. 'Of course you can phone England. Phone now. You will have to use this telephone, though. There is one in here because this is where I am for the greater part of each day. The only other one is in Armand's room in case he is contacted from the office. Use this one, *ma chère*. I have things to do. You will be private here.'

She began to walk off at once and Sarah felt very guilty.

'Céline! I didn't mean to drive you out of the kitchen!' Sarah just blurted the words out without thought and Céline turned, throwing her hands up in joy.

'You could drive me almost anywhere, Sarah,' she said happily. 'You have just called me Céline. Make your call. There is no hurry.'

She went out and Sarah realised just how much this meant to Céline. It had not been some whim that had had her father arranging this stay here. It had probably been his way of making sure that Céline felt she still had contact with him. Perhaps he'd known it would have the same effect on his daughter too.

Life was very strange, sometimes mixed up. At least she should attempt to get her own affairs straight and the best thing she could do was to phone Craig and make her peace with him. Until recently he had been very nice to her for a long time and she was beginning to feel very bad about the way they had parted. As usual, she blamed herself.

She phoned his flat and he answered almost immediately.'

'Sarah, love! I was beginning to think you wouldn't phone at all. I was wondering what had happened to you.'

'Well, the place is much further from Paris than I anticipated. It's in the north and what with one thing and another I haven't had the time,' Sarah confessed. She had been about to say that she had forgotten but she quickly changed that. It would have annoyed Craig.

'So when are you coming back home? I hope you've come to your senses now?'

Sarah's heart sank. He was back on the same old theme, thinking there was no need for her to be here. Theoretically there was no need; there was no gain from it, and that was how Craig looked at things, like a book-keeper, she thought in vexation.

'I'm staying for the month I promised,' she said and before he could answer she went on rapidly, 'Do you know it's a château? I'm actually staying at a château.'

'I don't want to know about châteaux,' Craig said sharply. 'I've seen one. Look, Sarah, if you'll allow yourself to think for a minute you'll realise that this is foolhardy. You're leaving your bookshop with somebody else and even if you trust her it's not the same as being here yourself. Things are sure to go wrong. In any case, it's time you were sorting out your father's affairs.'

'Oh, Craig! The lawyers will sort that out. I don't want to be involved with it.' Even the thought of it made Sarah unhappy but he didn't seem to hear that in her voice.

'You already are involved with it and there's no way of getting out of it. I expect everything's been left to you?'

'I don't want to know,' Sarah said quietly. 'Just thinking about it makes me miserable.'

'Then I'll have to sort things out for you,' Craig said briskly. 'Who else is there if I don't get your affairs in order?'

She could see an argument beginning to boil up again. This was the same sort of thing that Craig had said before. She knew what was in her father's will. She got a good deal of money now and the house where she had lived all her life. The rest she got when she was thirty or when she married, if that was earlier. Her father had set such a great store by marriage, which was rather sad in the circumstances. It reminded her of Armand's statement about marrying no matter what the consequences and she was inclined to agree with him.

'Are you still there?' Craig asked and Sarah realised that, once again, her mind had drifted away. She had been thinking about her father and Céline and getting the panicky feelings she had every time Craig pressed her towards marriage.

'I'm still here,' she said quickly, 'but I can't stay on the line for long. I don't like using other people's telephones.'

'If they live in a château they can afford it,' Craig pointed out sharply. 'What's she like, this woman, your father's—girlfriend?'

'She's very nice indeed and very kind!'

Sarah was angry at his tone as he spoke of Céline and now she wished she had never told him anything before she came here. It was only her fear that had made her mention the facts to him. If they had been as close as he seemed to imagine she would have told him even more and it was odd that she resented his remarks about Céline. She knew Craig much better than she knew Céline and Armand.

There had been a lot of love between her father and Céline. She knew it now even if she had not known it before. It was wrong to denigrate love in such a manner but she was beginning to realise that Craig denigrated many things.

'Look. Let's get things sorted out,' he said firmly. 'I'll have to be down at the club in a few minutes. I've got some special people coming round tonight.'

Suddenly, Sarah didn't want to know about his special people. She didn't want to know about any of the clubs he owned. They were noisy, too bright, too brittle, nothing that she wanted in life and they were Craig's very existence.

'I'd better let you go,' she said. 'You're in a hurry and I'm a bit embarrassed about using this phone. I'll try and phone you again.'

'Oh, no, you don't!' His voice suddenly hardened. 'Either you come home or I come and get you.'

'What are you talking about? You can't come and get me! I have no intention of leaving!' Sarah exclaimed angrily, shocked. Even though he had disapproved, he had never taken this attitude before and she realised now how vulnerable her father's death had left her.

'If you don't come back I'm going to come there. I want to see that you're all right, how things are.'

She knew that wasn't the truth. He wanted to pressurise her into going back and she knew that once she did get back there would be even more pressure. He would be talking again about marriage, a marriage she didn't want and had never wanted. She couldn't understand how she had got herself into the situation where he thought he had some hold over her, could force his opinions on her.

'I'm not coming back, Craig,' she said tightly and she knew at that moment that coming to France had been a very wise thing to do. It had given her time to stand back and see things a little more clearly. Her vague uneasiness had now become a concrete assessment.

'Then I'll be there the day after tomorrow!'

There was cold certainty in his voice that made Sarah gasp and she could imagine what it would be like if he turned up at the château. There would be trouble. Craig would make trouble and Armand would explode with fury if Céline's and his quiet home was disturbed by an outsider.

Armand was not really happy to have her here even though it was for his mother's sake and Sarah knew that he barely tolerated her. He would be alarmingly angry if Craig came.

'You can't come here! I—I'll meet you somewhere.' She was frantic that he shouldn't come and she knew he heard the alarm in her voice because she could hear it herself.

'Right!' he said in a grimly satisfied voice. 'I'll meet you in Paris the day after tomorrow. That place you used to stay with your father.'

Sarah remembered; a vivid picture came into her mind. It was a small hotel which she had been surprised to find her father frequented but it was so comfortable, so pleasant that she had been there several times. Of course, her trips there had always been with her father and she thought that this was a small cruelty on Craig's part, or maybe it was because he thought that she would miss him if they arranged to meet in some other place. It was second nature with her to give people the benefit of the doubt and even now she was doing it.

'I know the hotel,' she said quietly. 'How could I forget it?'

'Then I'll meet you there the day after tomorrow, lunchtime.'

'All right,' Sarah said wearily. 'But Craig, promise you won't do anything else. Promise you won't come here?'

'Not if you meet me, I can't let you be all alone, can I now?' he said coolly, and put the phone down. In spite of his words, there had been something threatening in his voice and for a moment Sarah stared at the phone, worrying. How had she got herself into this situation where somebody could order her about? How had she got mixed up in Craig's world?

She suddenly felt a great burst of relief when she realised that he didn't actually know where she was. She had never told him. She had expected to be closer to Paris and Craig probably thought that was where she was, somewhere close to Paris but in the north. She breathed a sigh of relief, startled that he had got her into this nervous state.

She would have to go to meet him and then she would make it clear that in future she would not be allowing him to dictate to her. She realised that she didn't really want to see him again but she knew he would react with fury to that. She would have to break it off carefully and step back into her normal life slowly.

She looked up, the worried expression still on her face, and was shocked to find Armand standing by the doorway looking at her. From the thunderous expression on his face she could tell that he had heard at least some of her conversation with Craig. There was very little doubt that he had heard the end, heard her pleading with Craig not to come here. She couldn't understand why it had made him quite so angry, but he was blackly furious.

He just looked at her and then turned and walked out and Sarah tried very hard to think back to what she had said over the last few seconds. She could not exactly remember her own words. She shrugged her shoulders in much the same way that Armand did. What did it matter? Soon he would be going back to Paris and she would not see him at all; probably she would have left before he came back to the château. She should not be worrying about what Armand thought. Her big problem was to get to Paris herself the day after tomorrow.

CHAPTER FIVE

ARMAND was very silent at dinner, broodingly silent, back to the man Sarah had first met. Conversation was very difficult but luckily Céline was in a lively mood, obviously still pleased that Sarah had called her by her first name, and, as she had no other alternative, Sarah brought up the subject of her trip to Paris.

'The day after tomorrow, I have to go to Paris,' she said, not daring to look at Armand. 'Is there somewhere near by where I could get a train?'

'Paris! *Ma chère*, you have only just come from there!' Céline exclaimed, but Sarah had to keep going now that she had started this.

'I know, but I'll only be there for a little while, as short a time as possible. There's someone I have to meet and I really must go.'

'Of course.' Céline reached across and patted her hand. 'Don't worry. It is easy enough to get to Paris the day after tomorrow. Isn't that when you have to go back for the day too, Armand?'

'Yes,' Armand said harshly. 'I will give you a lift, *mademoiselle*.'

'You don't have to do this,' Sarah said quickly and he glanced at her from beneath dark brows.

'And how will you get there if I do not take you?' he asked. 'How will you get back also if I do not return you to the château?'

'There's really no need to sound so annoyed about it, Armand. After all, Sarah will take up just a small space

75

in the car,' Céline pointed out and Armand glanced at her.

'Do I sound annoyed? I am not annoyed at all, Céline. I would be very pleased to take you to Paris, *mademoiselle*.' He shot her a look that was anything but pleased but Sarah had no alternative. She had to go and she had to quieten Craig down and get him to finally understand that she would do exactly as she liked and that no amount of pressure would get her back to England. She would stay here for four weeks, no matter what he said.

She went to bed that night rather gloomily and for a long time found it difficult to sleep, uneasy pictures of Craig coming to her mind, going over and over again the situation she found herself in, asking herself how she had managed to become so subservient.

She thought about the rather ostentatious clubs he owned. She hadn't known that at first. When she had first met him she had been quite charmed. He had been at a party given by one of her friends and his sleek, fair good looks had been the talk of the evening. She had been flattered when he had ignored the others and asked her out. The relationship had grown unexpectedly after that but she did not feel so charmed now. Sometimes she even felt threatened. With Craig she had stepped into a life she knew nothing of. She had always been rather sheltered and the glamour of it had been exciting at first.

She knew she was thinking about him rather frantically in order to keep her mind off Armand. The day after tomorrow she would have to face him all by herself and for a very long time. Céline had said that Violette De Brise was more of a match for him. More than some other woman? Did Armand have several regular girlfriends?

He did not have the look of a womaniser, but how did one tell? He was a thrillingly attractive man. Céline had not seemed to be exactly delighted at the idea of Violette and maybe she preferred one of the others. Sarah couldn't imagine Violette's face because she had never seen her. But she could imagine a woman in this house, a woman who had visited since she was a child, a woman who had a strong grip on Armand and who was very possessive.

The next morning was another bright, crisp day and Sarah was up very early, quite surprising Céline. After breakfast, when Céline was called to the telephone, Sarah walked out into the hall to leave her in privacy and she thought she heard the sound of horses. It excited her enough to make her open the front door and Armand was there, mounted to one of the horses she had seen in the stables. He was coming round the front of the château, heading towards the parkland, and Sarah just stared at him.

He looked magnificent sitting up there on the strong grey and his eyes met hers with no pleasure whatever.

'Good morning,' she said rather tentatively, fully expecting to be ignored.

'Good morning, *mademoiselle*. You are early today.'

'I—I thought I heard a horse and I came to look.' Sarah ran her gaze appreciatively over the horse and Armand fixed her with intent eyes.

'You ride?'

'Yes. I've always ridden. We always had horses at home. My father used to ride too.' For a moment, a look of sadness came over her face and Armand kept the horse still as it moved restlessly.

'How well do you ride?'

'Very well.' She looked up at him with no sign of boasting but with a look of certainty upon her face that must have convinced him because he turned the horse back the way he had come.

'You can ride with me,' he said shortly. 'Get changed.'

'I don't want to get in your way or be any sort of a nuisance,' Sarah said firmly. She was not going to be drawn into any sort of entanglement with Armand and she could already see that if she spent any time with him entanglement would come, even if it was only in her own mind.

'You will be no nuisance. You will be doing me a favour. There are, as you know, two horses. I can only ride one at a time and time is something I do not have. Change into something suitable and meanwhile I will saddle up for you.'

Even though she felt a little uneasy, Sarah could not still the look of pleasure on her face. She could hardly believe her good fortune, either. After last night she was sure that Armand would never speak to her again. He had left her with the feeling that she had forced her company on him for the trip to Paris when in actual fact she had been horrified at the idea of going with him.

She ran upstairs and found herself some jeans and put on a thick sweater and her jacket. As she was running down the stairs Céline came into the hall to tell her that she had finished on the phone.

'There was no need for you to have left the room,' she assured her but Sarah was smiling.

'I'm glad I did,' she said cheerfully. 'Armand is letting me ride one of the horses.'

'You can ride?' Céline looked worried and Sarah laughed.

'I've been riding all my life; in fact, I might be even better than Armand.' She tossed her head and Céline looked amused but she still urged caution. It gave Sarah a very warm feeling. She had never had a mother to fuss over her and, although she was well past the age when she needed it, she knew she was rather basking in the luxury of having someone worry about her.

She was smiling as she went through the front door and Armand has already saddled the other horse and was riding back, leading it with him. She had not expected to see him so swiftly and it almost wiped the smile from her face but she refused to be intimidated. It had been his idea. He had asked her if she wanted to ride. Come to think of it, he had almost ordered her to ride. She kept her smile intact.

'You are smiling,' he observed as he reined in and looked down at her. 'Riding pleases you?'

'It does but that's not why I'm smiling,' Sarah informed him blithely. 'Your mother was fussing over me.'

'And you find it amusing?'

'Not at all,' she said firmly. 'I'm not used to having a woman fuss over me. It's wonderful!' She mounted easily, not giving him time to help and as she swung the horse's head towards the park she felt quite pleased with herself. She had found a way to deal with Armand. She would overwhelm him with her own self-confidence. It brought an even wider smile to her face and when she looked she found Armand observing her silently.

'Are we going into the fields or across the park?' Sarah asked briskly.

'The park, unless you have other plans,' he murmured ironically. 'You may issue instructions if you wish.'

'I'll obey you,' Sarah assured him, giving him a haughty look. 'I'm sure if I transgress you'll point out the error of my ways.'

'This morning I am not sure that I would dare,' he muttered, slanting her a dark-eyed, sardonic look. 'You appear to be in a mood to conquer the world. Let us see if we can ride a little spirit out of both the horses and you.'

They were out on the drive and Armand turned suddenly, veering towards the trees, but Sarah kept up with him and set her lips firmly. She could probably ride just as well. Here was where Armand Couvier found himself equalled, or even bettered. If he thought she was too young she would teach him that youth had nothing to do with skill.

It was quite beautiful under the trees and Armand seemed to be content to hold his horse in, to pace along strongly, but Sarah was impatient. There were no long, open stretches of grassland here where the horses could run vigorously and she felt in need of a wild ride, something to clear all the confusion out of her brain. There was the same sort of tension in her that she could feel in the horse she rode. Beneath her it was waiting, restless, wanting to go and she felt exactly the same herself.

As they came to the edge of the park she saw wide fields, green with the grass of spring, and she cast a quick look at Armand, almost ready to take off without his permission. He was watching her, amused appraisal on his face.

'This is what you are waiting for, *n'est-ce pas*? I have felt you restless beside me, impatient as the horse you ride. *Eh bien, mademoiselle*; the move is yours.'

Sarah needed no further bidding; she took off, the horse springing forward beneath her with the same joy she experienced herself. She felt as she always felt when she was riding: not a care in the world. The sharp wind was whistling past her ears, her hair flowing out behind her, the hard pounding of the hooves like music as she bent low over the horse's neck.

It was a long, wild run before there was any sign of a hedge and Sarah narrowed her eyes, searching for any obstacles that might be in the way as she came to the high, thorny barrier. It was all clear; there was only further field at the other side and as she came towards it she gathered the horse in, ready for the leap. There was a satisfying pleasure at the sensation of bunched muscle and bone beneath her, the horse flying through the air as he took the obstacle like a bird.

She allowed him to run on and then wheeled round, smiling to herself, a feeling of triumph in her. She had never expected that Armand would refuse the jump and he had not, but to her disappointment he was not following her. He was already at the other side of the field, inspecting another hedge there and a piece of fence that seemed to be coming down. It was quite frustrating and she admitted to herself that she had wanted to get the better of him in a way that would leave him in no doubt about it.

As he turned she trotted towards him and then reined in to let the horses walk side by side and there was a little smile of triumph on her face.

'And how did you know, *mademoiselle*, that there was no ditch behind the hedge?' he enquired softly, not even glancing at her.

'Because I looked!' Sarah said smugly. 'I'm too experienced to jump a horse over a hedge and into a great big hole.'

Armand began to smile to himself.

'I wonder if the Valkyries as they ride through the heavens have dark hair or long hair the pale colour of yours?' he mused. 'I have never thought about it until today.'

'They're probably fair,' Sarah said smartly. 'And they're very dangerous women, not to be underestimated.'

Unexpectedly, he burst into laughter and dark eyes shot her a lightning glance.

'I have underestimated you? In future I will take care to remember that you are a menacing female with the ability to ride at breakneck speed.'

Sarah could hear the mockery but she was well-satisfied with events. She had made an impression, though she doubted if she had dented his masculine ego.

They rode for another hour and then Armand declared that he could spare no further time, and although Sarah was disappointed she had to admit that she had had a wonderful morning. In the stables she did the unsaddling herself and rubbed down her own horse, as briskly businesslike as Armand.

'Why do you keep the horses when exercising them is a problem?' Sarah asked when he had finished and was just standing there watching her.

'Like you, we have always had horses. It is not easy to think of getting rid of them. Besides,' he continued, 'Violette rides with me.' He suddenly moved restlessly. 'You amaze me,' he muttered.

'Why?' Sarah was startled into looking up and found him frowning at her, his eyes fixed on her intently.

'The way you handle horses. The fact that you have started a business of your own when your father was so wealthy. Even your stubborn determination to get to the village on your own two feet does not fit in with——'

'Oh! You thought I was a useless female, accustomed to lying around on the beach,' Sarah taunted smugly.

'Useless?' he queried softly. 'It is true I imagined you lying on a beach. However, I will not confess to thinking you useless. Even on the beach you would have your uses, even if only to give someone the exotic pleasure of looking at you.'

Sarah stared at him in confusion and then turned abruptly away. She had not expected that from Armand and she had no idea how to behave. She finished her task in silence and then turned around without realising that he still stood close behind her. She bumped headlong into him and gave a little gasp of alarm as strong hands came to her shoulders and steadied her.

When she looked up into his dark face there was a rapt look about him that would have held her fast even if his hands had not been firmly on her. For a second they stood absorbed and Armand's long fingers flexed on her slender shoulders as he stared into her eyes.

The beginnings of panic grew inside Sarah and his eyes became narrowed and alert.

'Once again you are afraid of the dim light and of me?' he asked softly and she quickly shook her head.

'I—I was just surprised, that's all.' To add to her confusion, his hands ran along her shoulders and partially down her arms, stroking over the soft wool of her sweater in a caressing way that brought a tremble to her legs.

'You are certainly not what I had imagined,' he murmured. 'I wondered if perhaps, like the flower, you were insubstantial. You seem to be all slender bones.' His eyes flashed over her face and the long, shining hair. 'I am beginning to see that the rose has thorns and certainly you have spirit. While I am away you will ride the horses for me, exercise them?'

Sarah had been contemplating her feet in confusion, alarmed at how she was beginning to feel, but his quiet request had taken the tension out of the situation and now she looked up with real pleasure on her face.

'Oh, may I? I'd love that!'

'It is not a gift,' he said, ironic amusement wiping away his deeply concentrated appraisal of her. 'As you can see, they are under-exercised. They need riding every day. It will be hard work.'

'I'll love it!' Sarah assured him radiantly and he nodded, looking at her thoughtfully before he let her go.

'You probably will. However, I will be concerned if I think that you are leaping hedges. When I am not there, do not behave quite so much like a Valkyrie. Keep the horses out for a little longer and run them a little less wildly.'

'I'll be perfectly all right and I wouldn't harm the horses,' Sarah said seriously. She had never been accused of being wild before and it was quite exhilarating, as if she had taken on a new character and was someone to be reckoned with.

'I require a promise.' Armand looked at her firmly, frowning as he noticed her expression.

'I won't leap the hedges and I won't be wild at all.'

'*Très bien*! Then I will go, leaving you with plenty of work to do. Who knows? I may even set you to cleaning out the barn.'

'I wouldn't mind,' Sarah confessed softly and she heard that low, dark laughter again.

'I think Céline would mind. I think there would be quite an uproar if I left you tasks of that sort.'

He walked out of the barn with her into the sunshine of the courtyard and glanced at his watch.

'I would imagine that my mother is about to serve coffee. She will be expecting you to join her,' he said briskly and Sarah knew she was being politely dismissed but she didn't want to go back to the warm kitchen yet.

'Are you coming for coffee?' she asked hopefully but he shook his head.

'No, I am not. I have plenty to do and time, as usual, is pressing.'

'When are you leaving?' There was a certain amount of wistfulness in her voice because now she realised that she didn't exactly want Armand to leave. She enjoyed being with him and now that she felt a little more sure of herself she quite enjoyed crossing swords with him.

'A week, perhaps. I doubt if I can spend more time than that. At the moment, Paris is taking care of itself; even so, I will have to make a trip in. If I stay here for more than a week, I will be getting endless calls and a variety of stupid and unnecessary questions. It is better to be there; besides, my life is there, if truth be known.'

He just nodded to her, walking away to the Land Rover, and Sarah went through the little gate and round to the front of the château. It was surprising that the sun didn't seem quite so bright when Armand was preparing to go. She shook her head in exasperation. This was no way to think. She was here only for a short time and then she would never see Armand again. In any case, she reminded herself, Armand had a life she knew nothing about. He didn't even know anything about her life, either, and besides, there was Violette and probably others. She had no doubt that he led an entirely different life in Paris.

She went into the house, forcing herself into the cheerful frame of mind she had been in before. Nothing must happen that would upset Céline. This time here was becoming important. Her father had thought this out carefully and he had been right. It was good for both Céline and herself.

Several times during dinner that night Sarah looked up to find Armand's eyes moving over her thoughtfully. She had no idea why, unless he was reconsidering his decision to let her exercise the horses. Céline made the evening a success with her constant conversation and it was only at the end of it that the very obvious reason for Armand's rather cold appraisal dawned on Sarah. He was back to disapproval because he was thinking about tomorrow and the man he knew she was going to meet.

She was thoughtful herself as she got ready for bed. Céline did not disapprove; nothing about her attitude had shown that anything was different. Of course, Armand had probably not told his mother about the telephone call he had overheard but, even so, it was none of his business.

She switched out the main lights and left on the lamps before going across in her bare feet to draw back the curtains and look out of the window. There was no sign of any storm tonight, just the moonlight, pale and cold. She had lost her fear of the darkness of the château and she knew that even if a storm came and the lights failed she would only have to keep perfectly still and someone would rescue her. She was beginning to feel safe here.

She turned to the bed and then stopped, her skin crawling in fright as a large spider ran across the carpet. Of course, it was only to be expected in an old house in the country but it was another of those things that Sarah found abominable. She made a dive for the door with very little thought behind her actions. It was precisely what she would have done at home. She would have rushed out shouting for her father.

She had the door open before she realised that now there was nobody to call for and she would have to deal with this herself. She could not get into bed and lie there wondering if it was going to climb up beside her.

Armand was just passing and he stopped to stare at her in surprise.

'What is wrong?' he asked quickly and Sarah felt all manner of a fool. Not only was she behaving like an idiot but she was now undressed, her robe not even tied.

'There's a spider in my room,' she said, hastily fastening the robe around her, her face reddening as the dark brows rose in astonishment. 'It's quite big!' she added indignantly. 'It went under a chair and I can't possibly get into bed knowing that it's there.'

Armand stepped forward, taking her by the shoulders and putting her firmly aside. His glance was sceptical and she thought he probably objected to her attitude.

'If you will permit, *mademoiselle*?' he murmured coolly. He might be angry but she didn't care at the moment. If he would deal with the spider he could go away and be angry all night.

He saw it immediately and pounced on it, but there was only alarm on Sarah's face when he turned to her with it cupped firmly in his hand.

'I have it,' he assured her seriously, his face bland. 'You wish to decide its fate?'

'Put it out of the window,' Sarah said earnestly, shuddering, and Armand walked across to obey. He put it out and closed the window before turning back towards her.

'You are not worried that it will whistle up reinforcements to advance upon the château in vast numbers?' he asked wryly, his lips quirking.

'I don't suppose it will survive that fall,' Sarah mused with a frown.

'It will. Spiders have many neat tricks. I will leave you to sleep safely.' He walked towards the door and turned at the last minute. 'You handle a horse much bigger than yourself and yet you are afraid of a minute spider?' His sardonic enquiry annoyed Sarah and she looked back at him angrily.

'A horse only has four legs,' she pointed out sharply and Armand stared at her as if he could not quite believe his ears. He had been looking at her as if he thought she had used the spider as an excuse to manoeuvre him into her room, but now he just looked astounded.

'If you consider it from that point of view, I suppose you are right,' he conceded. 'I am amazed that I dared to touch it myself.' He was grinning to himself as he went out and Sarah very carefully put all the lights on and walked round the room, searching to see if the spider had brought reinforcements in the first place. She was greatly relieved to find that it had not and when she got into bed she was almost too excited to sleep.

Everything about Armand stimulated her and, far from dreading the trip to Paris tomorrow, she was actually looking forward to it. She was not, however, looking forward to seeing Craig. If Craig wished to make a scene he was quite capable of making it in front of anyone and she knew she would have to be very careful when she met him. She certainly did not want the people in the quiet hotel in Paris to listen in as Craig raised his voice when she refused to go back to England.

She went to sleep with a worried frown on her face, Craig looming much larger in her mind than he had ever done before. Armand had said nothing but he had heard her speaking on the phone and he knew she was meeting a man in Paris and not some girlfriend. He probably thought it was someone she was so deeply attached to that she could not manage without him for a whole month. What sort of a person did that make her?

The following morning it was necessary to make an early start because, no matter how fast and skilfully Armand drove, Sarah knew that it was a three-and-a-half-hour trip to Paris. She would be lucky if she managed to get away without Armand saying something *en route* about her appointment.

When she looked out of the window she was rather disappointed to find that the crisp, sunny weather had gone. There was a lowering sky, not the sort of threatening sky there had been when she'd come to the château but a dull grey overcast of cloud that added a gloom to everything. She decided to wear the suit she had been wearing when she arrived in France. It looked cold and damp outside.

They set off after a very quick breakfast and Armand was silent as their trip began. This morning he was wearing a dark grey suit and a neat red and white striped tie against a stark white shirt. It shocked Sarah into realising that he was not just the person who worked the land that belonged to the château. She had never seen him looking like this and Céline's words about him now

had some meaning. He was the most disturbingly attractive man she had ever met.

He was concentrating on his driving, his brow creased
in a frown which Sarah assumed was because of some
problem at work. It put her back into the situation she
had faced before, where she was in a fast car with a man
who had no intention of speaking to her, but this time
she did not feel angry and she had no desire to quarrel.
In fact, she suddenly had the foolish wish that he was
going with her, to be beside her when she faced Craig.
It was an unlikely wish and she sighed, looking out of
the window as she said, 'The horses won't be exercised
today.'

'They will. I have asked two of the men to give them
a quick ride. It will hold them until we get back. They
normally have the job to do when I am away so it is not
unusual.'

'So you don't really need me to exercise them,' Sarah
pronounced in disappointment.

'Of course I do. You are an expert. The men merely
do it as a job and they would much rather be driving a
tractor. Horses know perfectly well who has the upper
hand and I suspect that they feel superior to the men.
You leave them in no doubt as to who is in charge.'

It cheered Sarah up. He was actually praising her and
she glanced at him secretly. He was not looking at her,
though. His eyes were on the road and he was frowning,
his mind quite clearly elsewhere. He had apparently said
all he intended to say.

Sarah was sitting in a sort of contented haze later when
he suddenly said abruptly, 'Where do you wish me to
drop you in Paris?'

'Anywhere that's convenient for you. I can easily get
a taxi to where I'm going.'

'I will drop you where you wish to be,' he said firmly.
'Once we are in Paris, whatever our destination, we will
proceed through a traffic jam. It is all one to me.'

'I'm going to a place just off the Champs-Elysées,'
Sarah said quietly. 'You could drop me off somewhere
near and I could walk from there.'

'I will have to collect you for the return journey,'
Armand pointed out with impatience in his voice. 'Tell
me exactly where you wish to go and I will take you. I
will then know where to collect you—unless, of course,
you wish to keep your meeting place a secret.'

She had no alternative but to give him the name of
the small hotel and she felt him stiffen beside her, his
face tightening.

'I will be ready to leave at four o'clock,' he informed
her coldly. 'I assume that this will give you enough—
time?'

Sarah's face flushed hotly. He could not have made
his opinions known more clearly if he had spelled it out.
She was not altogether naïve. He thought it was a lovers'
meeting and that some hotel would be necessary.

'I'm going there for lunch,' she said unevenly, and he
shrugged, dismissing her explanation.

'Your affairs are your own, *mademoiselle*. I will be
on time to collect you. Do not let that thought escape
from your mind or you may find that your stay at this
hotel is longer than you anticipated.'

It was the end of any pleasant companionship and
Sarah felt like screaming at him that he was wrong, but
she kept silent. It was nothing to do with Armand, after
all. He was a stranger.

When they arrived and she saw the blue and white
awning of the hotel in front of her Sarah felt utterly
downcast. She was dreading this lunch with Craig, expecting trouble, and now Armand was icily silent. He
had felt like her refuge but he was now almost an enemy.

'It's here,' she said quietly and he stopped outside the door, glancing up at the hotel.

'This is where your—friend is staying?' he asked harshly.

'No. This is just a convenient place, somewhere we both knew. After all, Paris is a big place and——'

'Quite!' he said shortly. 'I am sure you will both be comfortable here.'

'I have no intention of being comfortable,' Sarah said tightly, turning on him angrily. 'We chose this place because I used to come here with my father and it's somewhere that I know.'

His hands, which had been drumming against the steering-wheel, suddenly stopped and he looked across at her, his eyes angrily searching her face before he shrugged and looked away.

'I will pick you up here at four,' he reminded her coolly and Sarah nodded.

'Thank you.' There was lunch and then quite a long time afterwards. By four o'clock she would have seen far too much of Craig.

As Armand drove off he gave her a slight backward wave of the hand, not looking at her, and Sarah stood there with her own hands clasped together. She had not convinced him at all. He had dismissed her almost contemptuously.

Soon Craig would be here; in fact he might be here already. She would much rather have spent the time going round the shops. She glanced at her watch and found to her surprise that it was only eleven. Did Craig mean twelve or one for lunch? She had been much too agitated to press the matter when he had phoned.

She could not sit around the hotel for two hours. She suddenly brightened and looked around and as a taxi cruised by she flung her hand up. Why shouldn't she go shopping? She would give herself two hours and arrive back here at one. As far as she was concerned, that was lunchtime. If Craig was early, he would just have to wait. She settled in the taxi with a smile. She knew exactly where she wanted to go; Paris was not new to her and she knew exactly what she was going to get as a gift for Céline.

She enjoyed herself and found exactly what she wanted for Céline. It was expensive but that didn't matter; money had never been any problem. She had noticed how charming the red caftan had looked on Armand's mother and she bought her a cape, a beautiful tweed mixture with glittering colours woven into the red. It was beautifully packaged, too, and finally, with all her shopping under her arm, Sarah left the last shop and found a taxi. She had twenty minutes to get back to the hotel and that should be quite enough time.

Unfortunately, they ran into one of those sudden traffic jams that could happen in Paris and there was nothing she could do about it except sit there and wait. The hands of her watch were creeping towards one and then beyond it and she knew that her meeting with Craig would be stormy right from the first. He didn't like to be kept waiting.

CHAPTER SIX

CRAIG was in the foyer and as Sarah walked in he came towards her and he was not smiling. His smoothly handsome face was furious. It was twenty past one and her first thought was to apologise, explain herself, but she stifled that at the look on his face. She would make a stand now and not wait until she went back to London.

'Sorry I'm late but there was a traffic jam,' she managed breezily.

'Late!' he said in a low savage voice. 'I've been here since twelve.'

'But you said lunchtime. That's one as far as I'm concerned.'

'Possibly, in your social class,' he agreed with mounting anger. 'Where I was born it was twelve and we called it dinner,' he added nastily and unnecessarily. 'Where have you been?'

Right from the first he was being aggressive, taking an attitude. He wasn't even bothering to be polite and Sarah was angry, seeing, as she had done for some time, right behind the sleek good looks.

'I was here at eleven and as I imagined I had two hours I went to the shops. I've quite enjoyed myself.'

She said it defiantly and Craig's eyes narrowed.

'Maybe you have enjoyed yourself, in Paris,' he snapped, 'but don't try to pretend that you're enjoying the stay at this place with that French woman. I know you. You'll not be enjoying yourself, stuck in some little village out in the backwoods.'

'St Clair is a very nice little village,' Sarah said firmly. 'It's pretty and I'm going to go round the shops there. It was closed the other day when I went with Armand, but...'

'Who the hell is Armand?' Craig took her arm tightly and led her to the bar which, surprisingly at this time of the day, was almost empty. He ordered two drinks and then took her over to a table in the corner. 'Well?' he insisted.

'Armand is Céline's son.' Sarah sat back and began to sip at her wine. 'I came here to meet you because you threatened to come to the château. That's the only reason I'm here. You have no right to take this attitude with me.'

He looked a little startled at her tone and Sarah remembered that almost from the moment she had met him she had let him lead. That was how she had come to be in this situation now. Underneath it all he was probably as contemptuous of her as Armand was.

'It's just that I'm worried about you,' he said quietly and she knew it wasn't true. Now that she was looking at him in a different light, now that she had had time to stand back and think things over, she was seeing Craig as she had never seen him before. It was astonishing that she had ever gone out with him at all. She had been lonely, flattered and rather amused after spending a whole evening at a party where everyone thought he was Mr Wonderful.

He was not Mr Wonderful. There was a sharpness in his looks, a grasping air about him that she had never really seen clearly before. He was tensed up and she recognised it because she had been in that state herself very often. But he was not tensed up with anger. It was a sort of petulant anxiety. Something had gone wrong for Craig and she didn't know what.

As far as she knew all his business ventures were successful. The clubs were always full and made a lot of money. He had a very luxurious flat in the centre of London and he drove an Aston Martin. She couldn't quite put her finger on what it was about him but something was making him take an almost predatory attitude and she had the sinking feeling that she was the prey.

He calmed himself down and by the time he suggested that they have lunch he was back to being charming again, asking her about the château and the village she had almost seen, and Sarah was very relieved to talk normally and keep him in a good temper.

He managed to keep that up all the way through lunch. He talked in an amusing way about things that had happened since she had seen him last but it was always the club, this club, that club and the nocturnal world he lived in, which Sarah did not understand.

They sat for a long time, Craig talking almost incessantly, drinking a great deal of wine, while Sarah became more and more uneasy. She glanced surreptitiously at her watch. It was already after half-past two, and they were the only people left in the dining-room.

'Do you think we should move?' she asked and Craig snapped an impatient look at her.

'Why should we?' His voice was beginning to get louder and she thought uneasily about how much he had drunk. There were problems developing and she said the only thing she could think of to quieten him.

'Well, we don't really want anyone to know our business, do we? Maybe the waiters can hear.'

Craig shot an angry look at the two perfectly innocent waiters who were standing by to see if they needed anything else and as he turned back again the two young men looked sympathetically at Sarah. Even they knew that this was not a happy meal.

'We'll go back to the bar,' Craig announced and Sarah's heart sank. Quarter to three. It would be a long time before Armand came. She shook herself out of the state of mind where she was looking upon Armand as a saviour. He would come for her in a bad mood if his day had been unpleasant and in all probability he would drive off without her if she wasn't there on the dot. He had left her with contempt and he would meet her like that for sure.

Craig was in a truculent mood and Sarah could see herself being trapped in the bar with him while he drank even more. At this rate he would never make it back to the airport.

'Are you staying here tonight?' she asked and he shot her a leering look.

'You want me to book a room, sweetie?'

Sarah's face went angrily hot.

'I just wondered how you were going to make it back to the plane,' she said angrily, unable to hold her tongue. 'You've already drunk a lot. They're going to have to pour you out of the door into a taxi if you're not careful.'

'You'll get me there, love,' he said, leaning across to hold her hand. 'We can go back together.'

Sarah pulled her hand away and looked at him squarely.

'I am not going back,' she said sharply. 'I've hardly been here any time at all. I made a promise to my father and no matter what you say I'm going to keep it. I'm not going back. Get that firmly fixed in your mind.'

He glowered at her. His face, too, was rather red and she knew that whereas her colour had been from embarrassment his was from anger and too much wine. It came uneasily to her mind that he would also have been drinking while he was waiting for her.

'A month is a long time,' he pointed out in a hard voice. 'Plenty of things can happen in a month.'

'Such as what?' Sarah asked wearily. 'My affairs are going on exactly as my father planned it.'

'Why the hell can't you plan your own damned affairs?' he snapped in a sudden burst of rage.

'If you're going to be like this, Craig, I'll just walk out.' Sarah looked at him angrily but she was not as angry as he was.

'You'll not!' His hand fastened around her wrist but he seemed suddenly to realise what attitude he was taking. 'Look, Sarah, I want you back home with me,' he said more quietly. 'I miss you. Anyway, I had something to discuss. Do you want to be a part of a big business venture?' He made an effort to be cheerful, grinning across at her, but it was merely a temporary measure and Sarah knew it.

'Not particularly,' she murmured, relieved that the hard hand on her wrist had been removed.

'You'll want to when you have the details,' he assured her eagerly. 'I was thinking of opening a new club or extending one of those I already have. It only needs a bit of capital and you've got plenty of that.'

Everything in Sarah went very quiet. Was this what it was all about? Was Craig running out of money? With his fast lifestyle, was he stretched to the edge? Was that why he had been mentioning marriage for weeks and weeks?

'There's not much money I can lay my hands on at the moment,' she told him. 'Nothing is worked out yet.'

'Will you think about it?' he asked seriously.

'I don't know, Craig. I'll have to see what Daddy's lawyers say. They're supposed to advise me.'

'"Daddy's lawyers!"' he snapped in an unpleasant mockery of her words. 'If "Daddy's lawyers" had any sense they wouldn't be sitting in stuffy offices; they would be in business for themselves.'

'Not everybody wants a business,' Sarah said quietly. 'I don't. The only reason I have one is because I love books and I like to go and buy them, to browse through them. Otherwise I'd think of something else to do.'

'What about being the part-owner of a chain of night-clubs?' he asked jokingly, and Sarah shook her head, managing a laugh.

'That's something I never will be. That's your life, not mine.'

'If you married me it would be your life,' he pointed out, and once again Sarah had the feeling that she was fighting her way out of a situation that was doing its best to close in around her. She looked up at the wall where an ornate ormolu clock was showing the time—quarter to four! She almost sighed aloud. Soon Armand would be here. She made a great effort and smiled across at Craig.

'Oh, look at the time! It was lovely of you to come and see me,' she said cheerfully. 'I do hope we're not going to go on quarrelling. It's been pleasant having lunch with you and——'

'Oh, stop it, Sarah!' He was leaning back in his chair, looking very morose. 'You know damned well why I came and it wasn't to cheer you up, or anything else. I'll ignore the fact that you've neatly side-stepped my proposal again but I want you to come back. I need you.'

'For what?' Sarah asked and the sharpness in her voice attracted his attention. He glanced at her quickly.

'I need you around.'

She knew it wasn't true. He was trying to talk her into putting money into his venture and she had no intention of doing it. She had no intention of being involved with Craig in anything. She wasn't even sure that he didn't skirt on the edge of the law, come to think of it. There were plenty of strange-looking people in his clubs, many of them going in and out of his office, not just customers.

'I'll have to be going soon,' she said quickly and he sat up straight, staring at her.

'Why?' he asked in aggressive surprise.

'I had a lift here and I'm being picked up at four. I only came for lunch, Craig.'

He looked at his watch.

'It's damned near four now! What sort of a meeting is this?'

'Craig, I only came to have lunch with you and I've already been here a long time.'

'When you decided to arrive,' he snapped.

'I explained that. It was a mix-up.'

'Next time we'll get it better,' he muttered, apparently giving in, but Sarah's heart sank. As far as she was concerned there would be no next time. She would not ring Craig again and he did not know where to ring her; neither did he know where she was. It gave her a feeling of security because by the time she got back and the month was up she would have put a lot of distance between them.

She gathered her parcels and her bag, desperate to get out into the fresh air, and she stood, determinedly leaving him no option but to follow her. Once again the waiters looked with sympathy at her. She gave them a little smile. She wouldn't need sympathy soon, or, if she did, it would be an entirely different variety of sympathy because Armand would be here and she would be safe. If he was angry, at least it would be a civilised anger, not like this. Craig seemed to be barely in control of himself and she could never, in any circumstances, imagine Armand being out of control.

As they stepped outside, Sarah was startled to find that the overcast day had turned into a very foggy afternoon. There was even mist in the streets and she wondered anxiously if Armand would be on time. She didn't care about the fog once he was there. It was four o'clock and her heart gave a great leap as, exactly on time, the sleek silver car pulled up in front of the hotel.

For a few seconds, Craig didn't seem to realise that this was the person who was coming to take Sarah away but as Armand came forward it seemed to dawn on him that this was the last time he would see her for weeks and he grasped her wrist.

'Come back with me, Sarah! Let's have no more of this nonsense,' he said angrily. 'I need you!'

Her cheeks flooded with embarrassed colour. Soon Armand would be able to hear this even if he could not now.

'I am not coming back with you!' She said it in a sharp little whisper under her breath and Craig tightened his grip almost cruelly.

'Don't think you've heard the end of this,' he snarled. 'It's a lot of damned nonsense and you know it!'

Sarah felt almost weak with dread and then Armand was there, towering over both of them, too powerful to be ignored. He looked at her closely and then took her parcels, turning away to put them on the back seat of his car. That was when Craig suddenly grabbed her, kissing her almost furiously, and when he let her go Armand was frowning blackly as his hand came tightly to her arm. He opened the car door and Sarah was glad to slide inside. She was shaking and almost in tears.

Armand took one long, hard look at Craig and then said coldly, '*Monsieur.*' Then they were pulling away from the hotel as smoothly as a magician's trick.

Sarah couldn't help the long sigh of relief that came and she couldn't help her shoulders relaxing but she knew that Armand was in a wild rage. It didn't matter. She was safe. She had never felt quite so safe before. It was true that if Armand was a knight he was a black knight, but his strength seemed to be surrounding her and, right now, she needed it.

Thick mist was swirling around the streets. Already the rush homewards had started and although Armand took it in his stride she saw his lips tighten ominously. She had a good idea what he was thinking. Every bright light was hazed with fog, even in the heart of the city. Out in the open country it would be much worse. Over three hours of this would be impossible.

He never spoke to her and Sarah had no idea whether it was his concern about the visibility, the traffic, or his annoyance at seeing her with someone who had been, at best, only just about upright. Now that she felt safe, the embarrassment of it all was clinging to her like an unwelcome skin. She felt tarnished, as if by some means she had proclaimed herself to be a person exactly like Craig, and she suspected that Armand thought that with certainty.

They shot out on to the ring road and here there was even more traffic. As they passed over the Seine, the fog swirled up in thick clouds, sometimes crossing the road, and Sarah was not surprised when they saw a couple of accidents. Armand dropped his speed but not many were doing that and she heard him mutter under his breath as he had to take evasive action more than once. It became alarming, taking her mind off her other problems, and she was grateful for Armand's skill in handling the car.

When they left the city completely behind it was no surprise to see the fog thick and almost impenetrable. They slowed to a crawl but cars were still driving past with furious speed and at the first possible place Armand swung off the road to turn.

'We go back,' he said flatly when she looked at him with questioning eyes. 'I know this part of the country when fog decides to put in an appearance. We cannot reach the château tonight and we have two choices. We either go back to the city or pull into some unknown little place to find a refuge. I prefer to go back.'

He never asked her opinion but even if he had Sarah would have agreed with him. He could find a place to stay in Paris much more easily, and besides, he knew the city. It would not be some haphazard choice for an overnight stop.

On the return journey, they faced the same traffic all over again but Armand knew exactly where he was going and Sarah felt on edge. Since he had picked her up he had spoken only once, no more pleasantly than a taxi driver in the rush-hour. It would be almost a relief when he dropped her off at some hotel because she actually cared what he thought and his disdainful silence was making her want to hide away.

It was better in the lights of the city and, finally, the car nosed its way into a parking place by a huge building and as far as Sarah could see it was not some hotel. Armand got out and came round to help her but her eyes were scanning the tall building and she felt quite shaken when she saw that it was a block of apartments, an expensive block. Armand lived in Paris and she knew without him saying that this was where he lived. He was taking her to his apartment and not a hotel at all.

She said nothing as Armand took her arm and led her towards the great glass door but she was shakily impressed when he took out a card and inserted it into the narrow opening at the side, punching in numbers too swiftly for her to see. The doors slid open obligingly and, as they entered, a smartly uniformed man came out of a small room close by. There was obviously high security here and the feeling of unease simply grew.

'*Bonsoir*, Monsieur Couvier,' the man said very respectfully. 'The weather is keeping you here?'

'Unfortunately, Georges. Perhaps by morning this abominable weather will be gone.'

He did not linger to chat, even though the man looked with interest at Sarah, and she found herself in a rather ornate lift, speeding upwards with no other alternative.

'Is—is this where you live?' Sarah ventured as they stepped out into a carpeted corridor almost at the top of the building. She was nervous and it showed in her voice.

'It is,' Armand said shortly. 'I have a spare room. You will be comfortable. Or, if you prefer,' he added caustically as he opened the door of his apartment, 'I can deliver you to the small hotel where your friend is undoubtedly staying.'

'He's flown out already,' Sarah said, her face flushing at the tone of his voice. It was quite clear what sort of a meeting he thought she had had with Craig; she had not been mistaken.

'The airports will probably be closed down,' he rasped, showing her into a very luxurious drawing-room that opened off a square hall. 'I can ring and find out if he is there.'

'Please don't talk like that!' Sarah begged fretfully. 'I don't want to go to the hotel.'

'No?' He turned and looked at her with dark, narrowed eyes, his lips twisted in disapproval. 'Still, perhaps you do not. After all, you have already been there, *n'est-ce pas*?'

Sarah knew it was useless to protest unless she was prepared to beg for a hearing and some understanding and she was not about to do that. This was none of Armand's business. Craig was her own problem. In any case, Armand had no more right to take an attitude than Craig had. She was not some poor, weak-willed female to be ordered around. Even if she had been in the past, she certainly was not now and she was not about to let Armand hurt her with his acid words.

She walked across to the huge window that looked from its great height across the fog-bound city and then she turned, her face composed.

'If you could show me where I'm going to sleep, I'll get out of your way,' she said tightly as she found Armand's eyes on her with angry intensity.

'It is barely six,' he snapped, glancing at his watch. 'You intend to scuttle off to bed without food?'

'I'm not scuttling anywhere!' Sarah snapped back, her own anger beginning to rise. 'I just can't see much point in sitting down here and watching you glare at me!'

He continued to glare for a second and then turned away.

'The guest room is in here,' he told her abruptly. 'It has a shower-room and the bed is already made up. There is a maid who cleans daily. Food, however, is not brought in. We either eat out or make our own in these apartments.'

Sarah walked past him into the guest room and she could see that it was comfortable, as luxurious as the rest of the place. She turned to face him and kept herself very composed.

'Thank you,' she said quietly. 'It was wise to turn back in the fog. I won't be any trouble to you. I'm quite tired, as it happens.'

'I can imagine you would be,' Armand grated, standing in the doorway to stare at her scathingly. 'You do not look exactly built for a vigorous afternoon in some hotel. Even your boyfriend looked worn out!'

That was when Sarah hit him. She hit him with her flat hand, fury behind her action, and she felt only grim pleasure at the sight of the red marks of impact on the side of his dark face. The face darkened even more and before she could take any evasive action Armand grabbed her shoulders and hauled her against his hard and powerful chest.

'You little vixen!' he growled in a terrifyingly low voice. 'I will give you the satisfaction of knowing that nobody has ever done that to me in my life before. Do not think, however, that you are about to get away with it!'

His hand fastened tightly in her hair, jerking her head up to his and, in spite of her struggles, Sarah felt the hard pressure of his lips on hers. He was wildly angry, ignoring her murmurings of distress and there was no escaping the harsh punishment. She had been telling herself earlier that Armand would never lose control of himself but she knew that he had done that now and his rage frightened her.

Her head was spinning and she was hardly able to breathe; her struggles stopped because she had no strength to continue and Sarah went limp in his hard arms. She felt like a mouse, terrified, hiding, waiting for her fate, and she was so much withdrawn into her own self-protection that she didn't at first realise it when Armand lifted his head.

She took a great shuddering breath and looked up at him with wide, frightened eyes. Her lips were burning, her face white and shocked and she was trembling violently. For a second he looked down at her, his breathing harsh and uneven, and then his face changed; his dark eyes lost their angry glitter as they scanned her pale face. An expression of self-disgust flashed across his face and he took a long, deep breath.

'Forgive me,' he said heavily. 'I had no right to do that.' His gaze moved along her bruised lips as his hold on her slackened. 'I have never behaved like a barbarian in my life before, and yet I choose to behave like that with you.'

Sarah's tight, trembling fingers were still pressed against his chest and he moved them carefully, enclosing her hand in his.

'I have frightened you and hurt you. You struck out at me because I insulted you and you had every right to be angry. Forgive me, Sarah.'

Sarah was dazed at this apology, at his obvious regret. Seconds before, she had been almost afraid enough to faint and now she just stared at him with bewildered eyes.

'I—I only had lunch with him,' she protested in a whisper, 'nothing more.'

'It is none of my concern.' Instantly his face tightened and Sarah felt worn out, almost despairing.

'Oh, please!' she begged. 'Don't start all that again. I had lunch and I hated it. I was even late getting there because I went shopping first.'

Armand seemed to have forgotten that he was still holding her and his dark eyes scanned over her face, his hands tightening.

'He was drunk!' he said with distaste and Sarah nodded, feeling humiliated.

'Almost. It—it wasn't a pleasant afternoon.'

'And there has not been a pleasant ending.' He dropped his hands to his sides and Sarah almost fell. She was still trembling and his hands came back to steady her, resting against her shoulders.

'I did not enjoy seeing him—mauling you,' he said fiercely, his jaw tight with remembered anger. 'I did not enjoy either seeing him kiss you.'

'You imagine that I enjoyed it?' Sarah asked wildly and he stared into her eyes, his brows drawn together in a frown.

'You did not strike him. You have a hefty swing with your right hand but I notice he did not get the benefit of it.'

'I don't like scenes,' Sarah muttered wearily, trying to turn away. 'You have no idea what would have happened if I had struck Craig then.'

'Oh, I have,' he said savagely. 'He would have hit you back and I would have taken him apart. I was almost ready to do that without any excuse as it was.'

'But why?'

A rueful expression came on to the dark face at her bemused question.

'I am still wondering why. When I find out, perhaps I will tell you.' He suddenly relaxed and smiled down at her. 'Let us go out and find a place to eat,' he suggested quietly. 'If you had a bad time at lunch you will be hungry.'

He walked out, expecting her to follow, and Sarah went to wash her hands, her reflection in the mirror startling her because she did not look as shattered as she had expected. It was true there was a rather wild-eyed look about her but her face seemed to have come alive in some mysterious manner and she looked hastily away as she saw more than surprise on her face. She didn't look quite so innocent as she had done before.

When she went into the drawing-room, Armand was just making a phone call and he glanced round at her as she stood, putting on her jacket.

'I just remembered to call Céline,' he murmured, his eyes moving over her carefully. 'If she does not hear from us she will be worried.'

Sarah nodded but said nothing. Céline would be more worried still if she knew what had just happened. She was certain that Armand was also shaken by the result of his burst of temper. He didn't look quite so aloof and amused as he usually did and even while he waited for his call his eyes followed her.

Sarah went to take one last look at herself in the gilt-edged mirror that adorned one wall, her mind only just registering Armand's words as he told his mother about the fog.

'We will stay here for the night. Yes, she is perfectly safe.'

Sarah nervously inspected her image. Apart from the slightly swollen lips, she looked almost normal and she turned away guiltily as Armand put the phone down after promising that they would be back tomorrow.

'Shall we go?' His eyes came straight back to her and he walked slowly across to stand facing her.

'Yes. I—I'm ready.' Her fingers came nervously to button her jacket and she gasped with alarm as Armand reached out to touch her lips with gentle fingers.

'I am not always so brutal,' he told her softly. His fingers ran slowly along the still swollen length of her lower lip and his mouth tightened as she flinched.

'*Ciel*! Don't be afraid of me, Sarah. I know I have no right to expect anything else but I can be gentle.' His hand curved around her face, his other hand on her shoulder, drawing her closer, and Sarah began to murmur worriedly as his face came close to her own.

'Armand!' Her voice was anxious and he smiled into her eyes.

'At least it is making you say my name for the first time. Today you have had two furious kisses. One from me and one from him. Now I will show you what a gentle kiss is like.'

Sarah knew she should be struggling. She knew there would be no violence but common sense told her that she should try to get free, stand on her dignity, be angry. But with Armand's hand on her face and his lips hovering over hers she found it impossible to be angry and it was not fear that kept her still. It was the tremendous masculine attraction about him, the powerful ability he had to swamp her own personality. More than that, though, was the dreamy desire to know what it would be like if Armand really kissed her because she admitted that she had thought of it several times since she had met him.

His lips met hers, feathering along the length of them as if he was afraid that he would damage her further, and Sarah stood spellbound, quite unprepared for the sparkling feeling that such a tender caress should give her. He drew back slightly and she opened her eyes, looking up at him. His own dark eyes were hooded as he looked back down at her.

'Afraid now?' he asked. Sarah made no move and his lips came back to the corner of her mouth, this time a little more firmly.

She could not prevent the sigh that came from her and at the sound of it the hand that had been touching her face moved round to the back of her neck and his other arm tightened around her as he urged her closer. The kiss that had begun as a gentle salutation now deepened imperceptibly until Sarah no longer felt like a child being given solace, but a woman being kissed.

She had never been kissed like that before. There was something about Armand that seemed to enfold her completely and yet it was not completely enough. He was totally in control of the situation, holding himself aloof, and without any bidding Sarah moved forward.

His mouth became more determined, firmer and enticingly sweet, and a deep excitement began to grow that she had never felt before. His arms tightened and pulled her slowly against him and she felt nothing but incredible pleasure.

Something began to leap deep inside her, something she only vaguely understood. All she knew was that she felt no fear as Armand's hands came to her shoulders and as he gently slid her jacket away she was only vaguely aware of it. She felt his touch, warm through the silk of her blouse, and the pleasure against her skin was incredible. She murmured, but with no sign of distress and when his hand moved to cradle her head she found herself pressing willingly towards him.

It seemed to her that as their bodies met a kind of shock ran through Armand. It was something she instinctively felt and just as instinctively she would have withdrawn but both his arms slid around her, tightening her to him and his mouth began to move over hers more deeply in an almost secret exploration. His hand began to move slowly over her back and, as waves of relaxation spread through her, Sarah turned her face up even more, very clearly eager to be kissed.

She was quite unprepared for her own reaction and for Armand's when he moved one hand and cupped her breast through the silken smoothness of her blouse. The small cry she gave was not one of astonished outrage. Her mind told her it should have been, but the wave of feeling that swept over her took her completely by surprise. Her whole body seemed to come alive as her breasts surged to his touch; pained delight shot from them to her knees and her mouth opened almost in an act of joy to meet his lips.

A shudder ran through Armand's body, telling her quite clearly that her reaction was as much a shock to him as it was to her, and he moved her more tightly to him. The hand that had been gently cupping her breast now closed possessively around it, his fingers moving over the hard, erect centre as Sarah made a sound that could not be mistaken for anything but pleasure.

For a few seconds he held her fast, his mouth almost devouring, his hand moulding her breast, and then he drew back, his breathing undeniably unsteady.

'*Mon Dieu!*' He looked down at her with eyes that were burning. 'I am going out of my way to prove myself a villain.' He turned away, running his hands through

his thick dark hair. 'Put your jacket on, Sarah. It is time
we ate. At this moment, other people are a necessity.'

Sarah looked round in a daze, finding that her jacket
had slid to the floor behind her, and she bent to put it
on, struggling with the buttons with trembling hands.
He must have decided to take pity on her because he
turned and carefully removed her hands, fastening the
buttons himself and then holding her arm as he led her
to the door.

CHAPTER SEVEN

IN THE lift going down Armand said nothing and Sarah was still too bemused to feel any sort of embarrassment. He glanced at her as they were going across the foyer towards the huge sliding glass doors.

'You are all right?'

'Yes.' She quickly looked away, her mind going anxiously over what had happened. Why she had behaved like that. She had no doubt that Armand had merely intended to kiss her gently, an apology for his earlier violence, and she was quite sure that she had turned it into something else by her response. It was entirely her fault that he had kissed her and touched her like that.

She felt colour rising in her cheeks at the thought of exactly how he had touched her. Craig had once done that for just a second and she had been angry, alarmed and embarrassed. With Armand she had merely forced herself closer, letting herself be engulfed, wanting to be closer still. Even now she knew that the flush on her cheeks was not solely embarrassment. There was excitement there—the same sort of excitement she felt whenever she saw him. Now it had deepened and there was a sensuous awareness that she knew was not going to go away.

They went to a bistro close to the apartment. It was not a night for walking around. The fog was in the streets of the city, clinging to them, dampening Sarah's fair hair, and Armand hurried her inside to the lights and the warmth.

When the menus were brought Sarah looked at hers almost vaguely, not seeing the words. She had no difficulty reading French, just as she understood it readily, but now the words seemed to swim before her eyes and when she glanced up Armand was looking at her steadily.

He reached across and carefully removed the menu from her fingers. His eyes held hers and then he quietly went through his own menu, making suggestions of things she might like, carefully putting together a meal when she was so obviously incapable of ordering for herself.

Sarah dared not look at him, so she looked round the small bistro. Its atmosphere was very Parisian and once again she noticed how people came in and raised their hands in greeting to Armand although no one came across to speak. It was not that he looked forbidding but there was something withdrawn about him that would have kept anyone but the most intimate friends away.

Of course they would know him if he ate here often and Sarah began to ask herself if he came here with Violette. She decided it was more than likely, more than likely too that Violette stayed at the apartment. The thought brought a deep feeling of distress.

Armand too was silent and she was beginning to think that they would not be able to speak to each other at all when he suddenly said, 'Sarah?' She looked up at him, trying to keep her face cool but there was a warmth in his eyes that she found completely disarming. He reached across and took her hand, his own hand curling around hers, his eyes on the slender length of her fingers.

'Do not let what happened linger in your mind to embarrass you,' he said softly. 'Most women by now would be chatting away, the incident forgotten, but I know you are different.'

'I'm not different,' Sarah protested quickly, wanting to be like all the women he knew.

'You are.' His thumb absently massaged her wrist and then he looked up at her intently. 'It seems to me that you are several people: quietly determined when your mind is made up, capable but wild when you ride a horse but at other times so utterly innocent that I find it almost alarming.'

'You didn't think I was innocent earlier,' Sarah said, piqued that he should be treating her like a child, as if kissing her had been a big mistake. 'You assumed the worst when I went to meet Craig.'

'No, I did not really think that your assignation at the hotel would be for lunch,' he stated in a hardened voice, his hand withdrawn at once. 'Though I must confess, I found it difficult to imagine anything else.' His eyes slid over her face, his gaze penetrating and then he shrugged, going back to his meal. 'I have no right even to consider what you were doing. We do not know each other, you and I. When this month is up we will not even see each other again, so what does it matter?'

'It doesn't matter at all,' Sarah said, stifling the feeling that came over her at the realisation that in a very short while they would never see each other. In a small space of time, seeing Armand had become very important to her. She wasn't even sure how it had happened but it had. She had also become attached to Céline and could not imagine a time when she would not wish to see her.

With Céline she had an excuse to visit the château, to invite her to London, but as far as Armand was concerned she had no excuse at all. He was an outsider in this, someone involved unwillingly. When the month was up she couldn't see any possibility of meeting him without being very obvious, and she knew she would never be that.

The fog was still thick and heavy as they went back to the apartment and once again Sarah stood quietly as Armand dealt with the high-security entrance procedures and, once again, Georges appeared, his eyes even more interested as he looked at her. Now that it was quite late, it was obvious that Sarah was going to spend the night there.

'The fog is thickening you think, Monsieur Couvier?'

'Difficult to tell in the streets,' Armand murmured. 'It is too thick for any run northwards.'

'*Oui, monsieur*. It is best to be safely in bed.'

His eyes were still on Sarah and she found her cheeks getting redder by the minute. She had a great desire to tell him to mind his own business and Armand glanced across at her, noticing the growing displeasure on her face. His eyes noted too the way Georges was looking at her and he acted at once.

'But I have never introduced you,' he said with astonished regret. 'Georges, this is my sister; she is English.'

It would have been exaggerating to say that the man's mouth fell open but the suggestion of it was there and as Armand led Sarah across the shining foyer to the lift her own mouth tried to do exactly the same thing. She forgot her awareness of him as the lift doors closed behind her. She turned on him with nothing but astonishment on her face.

'Why did you say that?' She looked at him as if he had suddenly taken leave of his senses and he gave her an ironic smile.

'Georges was interested. It is quite obvious what his mind was running to. His mind can now run elsewhere. Believe me, he will spend the next couple of hours trying to work that out. When the night is over he will still be puzzled.'

Sarah found her own lips twitching and she glanced up at him in amusement to find his eyes steadily on her face.

'After all,' he pointed out softly, 'if my mother had followed her heart's desire, things would have been very different. I could have had a sister who would have been at least partly English.'

'Would you have liked that?' Sarah went on meeting the dark gaze and he shrugged.

'I do not think so.' He gave her a long, considering look. 'In any case, there would still have been you, *n'est-ce pas*? You were already there.'

'Thank goodness,' Sarah murmured and again she saw the quick flash of his smile.

'I agree.' As he opened the door of the flat he was still smiling but, inside, his amused mockery died away as he became very businesslike.

'I doubt if the fog will have lifted by early morning,' he mused. 'We may have to wait until lunchtime. With luck, though, we will wake up to sunshine and then we will get back to reality.' He left her and went to his own bedroom, coming back a few minutes later carrying a bathrobe and a pair of pyjamas.

'This is all I can offer you but at least you will be comfortable in the night. Let me know if you need anything else.'

'I'll be fine,' Sarah assured him. She took the bathrobe and found herself clutching a pair of pyjamas close to her. She wondered if they were Violette's but although they were silk there was a definite masculine look to them and a shiver ran over her skin when she thought of wearing Armand's pyjamas.

He was looking at her with amused speculation when she glanced up.

'They are rather big but you can always turn the legs up, or sleep in the top.'

Sarah mumbled her thanks and hastily made towards the bedroom, turning at the door to find him still watching her with a smile.

'*Bonne nuit*, Sarah. Sleep well,' he said quietly.

'Goodnight.'

His dark eyebrows rose tauntingly at her very stiff, English reply.

'I am to be called Armand only once during our association? I am disappointed. I imagined that we now had some unspoken agreement to be closer.'

Sarah glanced at him with a small jolt of surprise. She didn't want to be closer. It was pointless and dangerous. She disappeared into the bedroom, closing the door carefully as he still stood watching her, his eyes warm again.

Astonishingly, the next morning the sun was shining brightly and after breakfast they started for home at once. It was good to drive off in brilliant sunshine and Armand was in an easygoing mood. During breakfast in a small place at the other side of the apartments, Sarah had simply watched him as he talked to the barman and she had been fascinated to recognise that he was a laughing, sophisticated Parisian in this atmosphere and not the dark, reflective man she had seen when she'd first arrived.

She had become rather thoughtful, too, when she'd realised that instead of being insulted by the knowing looks the barman gave her she was excited. He assumed that she was Armand's girlfriend and the thought was not displeasing to her in any way whatever. She was quietly contented. This morning there was no lingering embarrassment or hurt. She knew also that she had got Craig completely out of her mind. When her month in France was up he might even seem to have been a figment of her imagination.

The traffic was not bad at all and as they sped northwards Sarah suddenly looked round at the back seat when she remembered that her parcels had been left there all night.

'They are safe,' Armand assured her. 'The car is alarmed and as you know the apartments are guarded, outside and inside.'

'For the very rich,' Sarah said shyly, making a point that his own wealth could compare with her father's.

'*Vraiment*!' He shot her an amused glance, following her thoughts well, and when her eyes went again to the back seat he asked, 'There is something precious back there?'

'I bought a gift for Céline.'

'She will like that,' Armand remarked quietly. 'She will know that you approve of her.'

'I didn't get one for you.'

He began to laugh, his white teeth flashing.

'It is hardly surprising. I know you do not approve of me. In any case, when I dropped you at the hotel yesterday I was in a very bad mood.'

'And when you came to collect me,' Sarah pointed out severely.

'The mood did not last,' he murmured and Sarah's cheeks felt hot. She was grateful that he did not continue that particular conversation although it was obvious that the thought of last night was in both their minds.

It was the first time Sarah had been so far north in the daylight and she looked around with interest. She could now see the sort of landscape that Céline and Armand lived in and she wondered how many times her father had been here. Had they met in Paris or had they come to the château when nobody else was there? In spite of Sarah's time here, the reality of her father's life with Céline had not completely settled in her mind. It

still seemed unreal and that feeling of unreality seemed
to edge its way into everything else.

Long before lunchtime they were very far north and
Sarah saw the rolling hills and densely wooded ravines
along the river valley that she had not seen before.
Everything was green with the green of England, the land
fed by rain. Today, in the sunshine, the whole scene lifted
her spirits and she was content to sit in silence, to admire
the churches, the abbeys, some of them beautiful ruins.
Many of the houses were quite grand even though they
were in the middle of farmland. This was a rich land.

'I wonder if I'll get to the coast while I'm here?' she
mused aloud and Armand looked across at her.

'You are asking me to take you? Why not ask
outright?'

'Because I'm not asking you. I know how busy you
are. I was thinking of going with Céline.'

She saw him grin to himself.

'I am busy,' he agreed. 'Also, in a week I will be gone,
but I will be back. A month is a long time. Wait for me.
I do not like to be left out of things. If the weather is
good we will have an outing to the sea.'

It was almost a promise and Sarah looked at him with
a certain glow to her eyes, forcing herself to look away
quickly when he gave her another of those lightning
glances. She was becoming a little too obvious and this
had happened so quickly. She carefully looked out of
the window and decided it would be best to remain silent.

She had suspected that Céline would fuss about their
stay in Paris and she did, endlessly, cupping Sarah's face
and kissing both her cheeks as if she had escaped something dreadful. She also shot several reproachful looks
at Armand, as if he had deliberately summoned up the
fog that had stretched from Paris to the English Channel.

It was not long before he went back to work and Sarah spent quite a happy time with Céline, springing the surprise of the cape on her. It suited Céline beautifully and she was as rosy-cheeked with pleasure as any girl. The thing that lingered in Sarah's mind, however, was the long look that Armand had given her when she had assured Céline that she had been comfortable and safe in Paris. His eyes had lingered on her even as he left, his expression enigmatic.

Things had returned to normal on the surface but underneath it all there was a burning feeling that refused to go. Sarah felt it all the time, a restlessness whenever Armand was not there, and she saw a similar look in his eyes every time they met. It was a hunger that was growing.

She exercised the horses herself the day after they returned. The men were only too glad to hand over the task and Armand was busy again. She only saw him at dinner and then he was preoccupied. She had expected that he would go off to dine with Violette and she could only assume that as he did not Violette De Brise was not yet home. The thought was in her mind most of the time and it added a rather tight expression to her face, even taking away some of the joy of her time with the horses.

She was leading one of them out the next morning when Armand appeared, pulling into the courtyard in the Land Rover and getting out to look at her sharply.

'Wait for me,' he ordered when Sarah looked away and made to leave. 'I got up an hour earlier today so that I could ride. I'm not about to be left behind.'

'You didn't need to get up early,' Sarah said huffily. 'There's no necessity to check up on me. I know exactly what I'm doing and if you don't trust me with the horses why ask me to see to them in the first place?'

'I do trust you with the horses. Though whether you know exactly what you are doing in any other direction is a matter of opinion,' Armand growled, looking up at her with exasperation as she sat on the horse and glared at him. 'I wish to ride with you and why this fact has brought on an attack of temper I cannot understand.'

He went to saddle up and Sarah sat in a bemused state waiting for him. It was unexpected, to say the least. His time was too valuable to spend just riding. She still suspected that he was keeping an eye on her. The thought of that and the necessity to control her feeling of awareness made her silent all the time and she did not gallop back with her usual shining eyes and smiling face.

She supposed it was her attitude that made Armand silent also and they never even spoke as they came back later and led the horses across the courtyard.

'I'll see to both of them,' Sarah offered quietly as they entered the stables. 'I expect you've left something very important to come and ride. If I do them both it will save you the trouble.'

She took off her jacket, hanging it on the edge of a door, and as she came back past him Armand grasped her arm.

'What is the matter with you?' he snapped. 'Do you dislike my company so much that you would prefer to ride alone? I notice that there is not the glow on your face today that was there yesterday.'

'How do you know?' Sarah asked crossly, pulling her arm to get free.

'Because I was watching you. I saw you making your usual spectacular leaps and I saw you ride back to the château. You do not have that same radiant look today.'

Sarah looked into his accusing eyes and her lips tightened with annoyance.

'So you *were* checking up on me!' she said angrily. 'Yesterday you were watching me to see how I behaved and today you came to have a closer look. If you think I'm not capable you can do the damned horses yourself!'

She turned away and reached for her jacket, determined to leave him with the grooming and unsaddling
too, but Armand spun her round, his hands tightly on
her shoulders.

'*Tiens!*' he grated, his eyes blazing down at her. 'You
bad-tempered little witch! Why should I check up on
you? I know perfectly well how you handle horses. Did
I not say that you were an expert? You imagine that I
am checking on you when I do not even check on the
men?'

'Then why were you spying on me yesterday?' Sarah
demanded, glaring back at him. 'And why get up early
to ride with me today unless you're checking more
closely?'

Armand's hands tightened painfully and she could see
that he was having difficulty with his own temper. The
desire to shake her was right there in his eyes.

'I was not spying on you,' he said with angry frustration. 'If you were not so innocent...'

'I am not innocent!' Sarah seethed, struggling under
his hands.

'Are you not?' he enquired scathingly. 'I confess to
watching you and your immediate thoughts are that I
am spying to see if you are up to no good. Any other
woman would not ask herself that question.' Sarah just
stared at him, still angrily, and he let her go, turning
away impatiently.

'Did it never occur to you that I merely wish to look
at you?' he asked harshly. 'Has it not even entered your
mind that I have more to do than take time off simply
to ride with you?'

'Then why did you?' Sarah looked at him with bewildered eyes. Even his back looked angry and what he
was saying to her just didn't sink in.

'Because I wanted to be with you,' he snarled, turning
on her suddenly. '*Mon Dieu*! You are truly innocent.'

He stared at her almost resentfully. 'Yesterday I did not spy. I merely watched you. I *wanted* to watch you! I *like* to watch you!'

Sarah just looked up at him in the dim light of the stables and after a second his anger faded; his hand came to her face and he ran his fingers gently down her cheek.

'Hair like the moonlight, a skin like silk, eyes like a fawn and yet it never enters your mind that I may wish to stop what I am doing and simply look at you.' His lips twisted in a bemused smile. 'Deep down, you are afraid of me and yet you watch me too, inviting my attention.'

Sarah blushed and turned her face away, unable to cope with the moment, but he cupped his hand around her cheek and turned her back to face him.

'You want my attention?' he asked softly. 'You have it, *petite*.'

When she just looked back at him helplessly, he drew her slowly into his arms, his eyes running along the soft outline of her lips.

'You have my undivided attention,' he murmured as his mouth captured hers. He was not holding her too tightly, but immediately sensations began to melt through Sarah, making her weak. As his mouth moved gently over hers she relaxed, moving against him, and, as it had done before, the touch of their bodies together ignited flames.

Armand tightened her to him possessively, his hand tilting her face closer as his tongue ran along her lips. She knew the silent command even though she had never felt it before and her lips parted willingly, allowing him to deepen the kiss. He groaned low in his throat and her hand against his chest felt the strong racing of his heart. Her own heart felt like a wild butterfly, struggling to be free, and with a little moan she pressed herself closer, her arms winding around his neck.

'This is madness and we both know it,' Armand muttered unevenly, his lips trailing kisses across her arched neck. But Sarah took no heed of either his words or the small voice of warning inside her. She gave a tiny, whimpering cry and turned her face to search for kisses that were instantly given.

It seemed to be the signal for an explosion of sexual need. Armand's body hardened against her own, his hands sliding down her back, urgently pressing her closer with no thought of restraint, and Sarah clung to him with the same urgency, her body soft and open to him until he had no need to hold her.

When his hands slid to her waist and then upwards to cup her breasts with the same possessive demand that had been in his kisses, there was no mistaking the swell of her breasts under his searching fingers, no mistaking the gasping cry of delight that was almost torn from her dry throat.

'Armand!' She almost sobbed his name and he relented, his arms moving to hold her close, unwilling to let her go.

'*Dieu!*' he groaned, his face buried in her hair. 'I am mad and I know it. But you——' he looked down at her with blazing eyes '—you do not even recognise danger. Do you know that I want you and could take you now? Do you?'

He stared into her dazed eyes and then kissed her hungrily, his grip on her waist almost cruel, his power forcing her head back. It was a kiss of need and frustration and then he reluctantly let her go, turning away from her, his chest heaving with the effort it took to curb such stormy emotions.

'You offered to see to both horses,' he grated. 'I am taking you up on that offer because if I stay here for one more second you will no longer be burdened with such innocence.'

He walked out and Sarah leaned against the door of the stall, her breath fighting to steady, her hands clutched beneath her breast. She was not the innocent he thought. She had been well aware of the consequences of her actions. Armand seemed to imagine that she was totally unsuspecting, a ready-made prey, and she felt a stirring of some deep emotion that he had not been prepared to take advantage of her, just as he had not taken advantage of her at his apartment.

It might be that he cared too much about his mother and what she would think, but Sarah felt a spark of hope that this was not the only reason. He protected her, even from himself. And she had needed it because with Armand she had no means of protecting herself. She wanted him and it had been in the air almost since her first glimpse of him at the airport. His stormy darkness, his compelling eyes and his superb masculine grace set up a racing inside her that nothing would quell and when he touched her she just let the whole thing devour her as Armand had wanted to do.

She had looked for some spark of feeling when she had first known Craig, instinctively knowing it should be there. Where had her instincts been when she had seen Armand that first time? She had felt a shock, been compelled to look back at him when common sense had told her to look away. The spark had been there from the first but she had not recognised it.

She took a sighing breath and then turned to the horses. It was safe to stand and let her emotions run riot here in the dark stables but she still had to face Céline and Céline was no fool. She also had to face Armand tonight at dinner.

He was not there at dinner and Céline said, with no sign of pleasure on her face, that Armand had gone to meet Violette in the village.

'He is dining tonight with Violette and her father,' she said with tightened lips. 'Now that she is home, we shall see very little of Armand.'

Sarah had known it, but all the same she had to stifle the burst of hurt that came suddenly. Armand would keep out of her way in future and it was more likely that he suffered no frustration at all with Violette De Brise.

He had still not returned when Sarah went to bed and she opened the curtains when her lights were safely extinguished. Once again there was the pale, cold moon, the darkened landscape, the stillness and quiet of the old château. It was astonishing how quickly this place had become established in her heart.

Whatever had happened to her she was not going to be happy. Armand would return to Paris and she would never see him again. He had spoken of coming for a weekend but she knew that now he would not. She had thought him brooding and cold but now she knew differently and he would make the sensible decision to be as far away as possible until she had gone.

If she were wise she would be glad of that decision. But she was not wise. Any common sense would have to come from Armand. Maybe she was as innocent as he thought.

The next day, Céline wanted to go into St Clair to the shops and she invited Sarah to accompany her. After exercising the horses, hoping pointlessly that Armand would appear, Sarah was very downcast and she readily agreed to go. Céline had her own small car and immediately after lunch, when Armand again did not appear, they set off to the village.

Normally, Sarah would have been excited, looking forward to the small treat, but her life seemed to have been altered totally by her feelings about Armand and she had to make a great effort to be cheerful and respond to Céline's chatter. It was another cold, sunny day—not cold enough to stop the men who were playing *boules* in the square, though, and they greeted Céline cheerfully although mostly their eyes were inquisitively on Sarah.

'You are an event in this small place, *ma chère*,' Céline laughed as they went to the bread shop. 'Even the old men are interested. By now, of course, the whole village will know that an English girl with dazzling hair is staying at the château. There is a sort of bush telegraph in these parts and even if there had not been Mathilde is so taken with you that she will have been proudly boasting.'

'Any outsider would be an event here, I imagine,' Sarah suggested and Céline agreed.

'True, *ma chère*, true. But to get the men to look up from their game of *boules* takes an extra something—like very fair beauty. That is what you have.'

'Did they know about my father—in the village, I mean?' Sarah asked carefully but Céline was not one bit put out.

'They did not. My business is my business. Besides, John and I never came here. We had a house on the coast. I did not want to share him, even with my ancestors—you understand? It was not discretion. It was more a desire to keep him to myself.'

Sarah nodded. She understood. It had been a secret life, and curtailed because of the secrecy. She felt very sad for them and she agreed more than ever with Armand. They should have married.

'Oh, *why* didn't you get married?' she asked sadly. 'So much life wasted!'

'It was not wasted, Sarah,' Céline murmured, tucking Sarah's arm affectionately in her own. 'It was precious. Also there was Armand's father. He was a powerful man with a great deal of influence. Because I was not prepared simply to bow to his every whim he hated me, I think. He would have found a way to strike back, probably at Armand. There was also you, *ma chère*. We also took that into consideration, John and I.'

'I wouldn't have minded a bit of mothering,' Sarah muttered. 'It would have been good to have you to turn to, another woman to tell my problems to.'

'And Armand would by now have almost been a brother. You would have liked that, too?'

'I—I don't know.' Sarah confessed hastily, knowing that she would not have liked that at all. Céline gave a little smile but said nothing else and they spent a very interesting time going round the few shops and visiting the small market that was set up at the side of the square.

It served to cheer Sarah up and they were just returning to the car when she felt Céline stiffen somewhat.

'You are about to meet Violette,' she said quietly. 'There is no alternative as she seems to be set on the idea.'

Céline's voice had taken on a rather sharp quality and Sarah knew then for sure that Armand's mother did not particularly like his choice of a future wife. As Céline had said, however, there was no way of getting out of it, because a beautiful and vigorous woman was approaching across the square with no intention of being side-tracked and Sarah steeled herself to meet the woman who was part of Armand's life.

Violette De Brise was tall and dark, the same sort of darkness that was visible in Céline and Armand. She was part of the place and she looked it, her self-assurance making Sarah feel almost tired. There was a definite air of determination about her as she bore down on them and Sarah had just enough time to notice her good figure and her stylish clothes when Violette almost pounced on Céline.

'*Madame*! It is so long since I saw you.' She greeted Céline effusively, kissing her cheeks and expecting the same sort of welcome. She received it but much more coldly, Sarah noted, and then it was her turn. 'This is your friend from England?' Violette enquired with a smile at Sarah that did not reach her dark eyes. 'My father was telling me that he had met her. She does not speak French.' The last was said with some satisfaction and Céline laughed.

'She does. At least, she understands it perfectly and reads it, too. She has not had the opportunity to speak the language very much, though, and Armand and I converse in English. Perhaps we could do that now, Violette?'

'But of course, *madame*,' Violette agreed when they had been introduced. 'You are here for a short time, *mademoiselle*?' she enquired in English.

'A month,' Sarah was pleased to inform her. 'Céline and I want to get to know each other really well.' She deliberately used Céline's name, having noted that Violette did not, and she supposed that it was a childish trick but she wanted to gain some superiority over this woman who watched her with a smile on her lips and irritation in her eyes.

'A month? It is a long time,' Violette said sharply. 'The time of the year is also not very exciting. A strange time for a holiday.'

'I'm not really on holiday,' Sarah informed her quietly. 'Céline was a dear friend of my family. Now that I'm alone I wanted to get to know her better. As to the time of the year, I love it.'

CHAPTER EIGHT

LATER as they made their escape, Céline was laughing quietly.

'Very well done, *ma chère*,' she murmured as they got into the car. 'You have a lot of spirit for a girl who is afraid of storms. Violette does not, I think, relish the idea of your staying at the château, so close to Armand. You are just a little too beautiful to be ignored. Thank you too for saying that I was a friend of your family.'

'You were the dearest friend of the only family I had,' Sarah assured her quietly and Céline bit her lip to stop the flood of emotion.

'Already I am very fond of you, Sarah,' she confessed softly. 'Be careful, or I may wish to keep you here.'

'And what about my shop?' Sarah laughed. 'I can't afford to be kidnapped.'

'Then we will pay visits, frequently!' Céline announced and Sarah smiled, snuggling into the warmth of the little car.

'Before I go we'll work out a timetable,' she promised gladly. 'You'll love my bookshop and I still have the house where my father and I lived. I'll never sell it. You can come to stay there with me.'

'I will like that very much. There will be things to remind me of John and I will discover things about him that I never knew. You can talk to me about his life.' At that moment, Sarah felt very close to Armand's mother and she blessed her father's loving decision.

Apart from the unwelcome intrusion of Violette, it had been a happy expedition and they arrived back at the château laughing and talking animatedly. Their smiles died, however, as they were met at the door by Mathilde.

'She is doing it again, *madame*,' Mathilde stated severely, her eyes fixed on Céline with mounting disapproval. 'Madame Delaine has had the doctor phone the château for her. She is having another attack.'

'Oh, *mon Dieu*!' The smile died from Céline's face and she rushed inside, thrusting her shopping into Mathilde's ample arms. 'How bad is it, Mathilde?'

'It is much as usual.' Mathilde was frowning blackly and Sarah couldn't understand her attitude when somebody that Céline knew and cared about was obviously ill. 'You are going, *madame*?' Mathilde asked sharply and Céline looked at her rather pitifully.

'But what else can I do, Mathilde? You know how it is.' She glanced at Sarah apologetically and ran up the stairs as Mathilde almost stamped into the kitchen to dump the shopping. Mathilde was muttering to herself angrily and Sarah decided to stay out of it for the moment. She went to put her own small amount of shopping in her room. It was puzzling but no doubt Céline would explain later.

When she went down, she could hear Armand's voice in the kitchen. The language was too swift for her to follow but the tone was clear. Armand was displeased and Mathilde was putting in her twopenny-worth. Sarah dived into the small salon to get out of the way and stayed there until she heard Céline coming down the stairs.

To her astonishment, Céline had changed and packed a case and she carried it to the kitchen as Sarah joined her. They did not get there, however, because Armand had also heard his mother approaching and he appeared at the kitchen door with a darkly furious face.

'*C'est incroyable*!' he rasped, glaring at his mother. He stood with his feet planted and his hands on his hips and just threw words at Céline, words that Sarah could not understand but which she felt were very savage. He was quite alarming but Céline was not at all alarmed.

'If you wish to remonstrate with me, then do it in English,' she insisted sharply. 'Sarah is here and this is not polite.'

Armand glanced at Sarah with the same near-violence in his expression and then he turned back to his mother.

'Polite? I do not have the patience for politeness at the moment! How many times will you allow that woman to pull this trick?'

'Armand, your aunt Martine has had a heart attack——'

'Again!' he interrupted with angry exasperation. 'How does she get away with this? You know she is simply bored and wants your company. Tell her to come here—after I leave!'

'I cannot ignore her,' Céline protested, waving her hands about in agitation. 'This time it may be true. It was the doctor who phoned.'

'He phoned the last time,' Armand reminded her frustratedly. 'No doubt she has him as utterly at her mercy as she has you.'

'Perhaps, but I must go and see for myself,' Céline said stubbornly, holding her own with no sign of giving ground.

'And what about Mademoiselle Thorpe?' Armand queried savagely. 'She has given up a month of her time to be with you.'

'I know this.' Céline looked at Sarah worriedly. 'I cannot ignore this call from Martine. I will be gone for just a short time but I must go all the same. Forgive me, Sarah, but...'

'Don't mind me,' Sarah said hastily. 'I can go home,' she added, but she was startled at the effect that this had on everyone.

'No!' Céline, Armand and even Mathilde said it in unison. Sarah just looked at them in surprise but it was Céline who spoke.

'I will be back as soon as possible, perhaps even to-morrow. Please stay, Sarah. I'm sure that Mathilde...'

She looked hopefully at Mathilde but she got very little approval; Mathilde deliberately turned and started to pack away the shopping, committing herself to nothing at all.

'Do you wish me to take you there?' Armand asked in an impatient voice but Céline shook her head.

'I will drive myself. It is a short way to the coast. I can then get away quickly when she feels better.'

Armand made no further comment but he took Ceéline's case and walked out to her car. He was bristling with rage and Sarah was too confused to consider her own situation in this small drama.

'You will stay?' Céline asked a little anxiously, smiling when Sarah nodded. 'Mathilde is annoyed at the moment but she will come round when I have left,' Céline continued in a low voice, her eyes on Mathilde's disapproving back. 'She will cook. Do not worry.'

Sarah was not worried. She was more than capable of cooking any meal and for now she had not time to think beyond the moment. She realised the significance of the new situation when Céline swiftly pulled away from the door and Armand came back in as his mother's car tore down the drive.

He looked too annoyed to speak but he obviously thought it necessary and he stood in the doorway of the kitchen and glared at Sarah with irritated dark eyes.

'Now what do we do?' he asked in a harsh voice. 'I assume you have thought of the consequences of my mother's mission of mercy?'

She hadn't, but she was surprised to see him take this hard attitude.

'Well, surely she had to go? I mean, if your aunt——'

'Martine Delaine is not my aunt,' Armand stated in disgust. 'She is an old friend of my mother. *Ciel*! If I did not know better I would believe I had enough aunts to fill the château. None of them, however, is in any way like Martine.'

'But—but a heart attack...?' Sarah pointed out quietly, looking a little reproachfully at him for his lack of consideration.

'She has heart attacks approximately six times in a year,' he assured her caustically. 'Madame Delaine lives alone and is very happy to do so. From time to time, however, she craves company—Céline's. She then has an attack and it continues until she is bored with the event.'

Mathilde chipped in rapidly, outrage on her face and, as she finished and went back to her tasks, Sarah looked enquiringly at Armand. He was almost grinning, much to her surprise.

'Mathilde shares my feeling of annoyance,' he stated, glancing at Sarah with growing amusement. 'She says that Madame Delaine is too old for this sort of trick and thinks that she will do it once too often——'

'Crying the wolf at her age!' Mathilde interrupted in an outraged voice. 'One of these days...'

She turned away on that dark statement and Sarah understood their annoyance. It suddenly dawned on her, too, that there was more to think about than cooking the dinner.

'Oh!' she exclaimed, biting at her lip, her eyes moving anxiously to Armand's face. 'But what about...?' She glanced at Mathilde's back and lowered her voice. 'What about...?' Faced with it she couldn't quite come out with the words but it had dawned on her that there would now be only Armand and herself here tonight.

'Ah!' Armand looked down at her with a frown. 'You begin to see the problem, I assume? Perhaps your generous nature is not now quite so comfortable with events?'

'I should have offered to go with her,' Sarah said worriedly but he merely snorted angrily and turned away.

'*Mon Dieu*! With you there also she would have been confined to her bed for weeks. Her excitement at an English visitor may even have brought on a real attack. She will dismiss my mother when she becomes bored. I cannot imagine her ever becoming bored with you and Céline would be there indefinitely.'

'Then what ... ?' Sarah felt like wringing her hands. It was pretty silly but she knew that Armand did not approve of there being no chaperon, even though he had taken her to stay with him in Paris. Here, of course, people would talk.

'Oh, I am sure that Mathilde will be willing to stay the night in the château,' Armand said easily, his eyes amused on Mathilde's back.

'I will see,' she muttered without turning. 'I have a husband, do not forget.'

'I'll cook the dinner,' Sarah offered quickly to placate her but it had the opposite effect.

'*Non*! It is not right!' Mathilde turned round, stung into action. 'You are a guest and, in any case, you are very slender, delicate. I will cook until *madame* returns.'

'Obviously she has not seen you handle the horses in your delicate way,' Armand murmured, taking Sarah's arm and urging her out of the kitchen. 'She appears to think you are a weak and shaking female.'

Sarah flushed hotly. She was a weak and shaking female when Armand touched her; until then she could hold her own with the best of them. He led her to the salon and poured her a drink.

'Have a glass of wine,' he suggested as he handed it to her. 'It will help you to face the harsh reality of Céline's desertion.' He looked down at her with ironic eyes as she perched on a chair and Sarah did some rapid thinking.

'I could just go home,' she mused. 'It would solve all the problems.'

'And break the promise to your father,' Armand pointed out. '*Pas question*! We will manage. Mathilde will cook and stay until the meal is over. She will then clear away and you will go to bed early like a good little girl. That way we will rarely see each other. The situation will be normal.'

'Hardly that!' Sarah said crossly. 'Mathilde will be working all hours. She has her own home and a husband, as she pointed out.' She suddenly brightened and looked up. 'I know! I'll help with the cleaning!'

'You will not!' Armand glared at her, his derision vanishing. 'You will carry on as normal. You did not come here to be a servant.'

'Well, I'm already a stable-hand,' Sarah reminded him slyly and his face darkened with anger before he realised that she was mocking him.

'I can always withdraw the privilege,' he warned. 'And back to serious matters,' he continued when she looked alarmed at the thought of her morning ride being discontinued. 'You will not clean the château. You will remember that you are a guest. Otherwise there will be trouble.'

'I can handle trouble,' Sarah stated haughtily and he stared at her intently before deliberately letting his eyes roam over her figure.

'Can you?' he asked softly. 'I have seen no evidence of it. What you can handle, *mademoiselle*, is a horse. Continue to do so and do not go for bigger game. The *horses* are impressed by your experience.'

Sarah looked away rapidly. He was pointing out, with little subtlety, that although she was experienced with horses she was not experienced with men, especially with a man like him. He had clearly got over his moment of madness after some time with Violette. Unfortunately, she had not got over hers. She murmured incoherently and escaped to her room.

Dinner was safely managed because Armand was blandly polite and Mathilde pottered in and out serving, much to Sarah's embarrassment because she felt utterly useless. It became obvious too that Mathilde had no intention whatever of staying at the château overnight and as they drank coffee and Mathilde dealt with the dishwasher Sarah voiced her alarm.

'Are—are you going out tonight?' she asked uneasily.

'And leave you here alone?' Armand looked across at her, his ironic amusement turning to quiet reassurance when he saw the look on her face. 'No, I am not leaving the château. You can sleep safely.'

'Thank you,' Sarah murmured, her shoulders relaxing.

'I do not like you to be afraid,' he said quietly. 'The spider was amusing but I would not be amused if I thought you were lying in your bed terrified.'

Something in his voice drew her attention and she looked up quickly to find his serious gaze on her.

'I—I won't be afraid if you're in the château,' she managed carefully, answering his unspoken query.

'Then it is my turn to say thank you,' he assured her softly. 'Perhaps it would be a good idea to go to bed now?'

'Like a good little girl?' Sarah asked a trifle huffily and he gave her one of his slow, ironic smiles.

'Like a *wise* little girl,' he corrected in the same softly derisive voice. It was enough to send her hastily to her room.

In spite of Armand's orders, when Sarah had finished with the horses the next day, she came back and proceeded to wheedle her way round Mathilde on the matter of cleaning. She pointed out that, with *madame* away, she had nothing to do and would be bored and lonely. It was in fact true. The whole day stretched before her because she knew that Armand would stay out as long as possible and was keeping out of her way.

Some really efficient cajoling was necessary but over coffee with Mathilde Sarah kept up the pressure and finally it was agreed that she could do her own room and her own bathroom today. After that, Mathilde insisted importantly, she would think about things.

Actually, Sarah enjoyed herself. There had never been any necessity for her to do housework and the novelty was quite invigorating. It was also satisfying to put a shine on furniture and she came down the stairs later with a bright scarf round her fair hair and the brushes and cleaner in her arms. She was smiling happily but the smile died and guilt rapidly took its place as she found Armand standing in the hall watching her descent. He was wearing jeans and high boots, a black sweater and jacket and his frown was equally black.

'I can see that you are quite prepared to get your own way by stealth if you are not able to get it otherwise,' he rasped. 'I told you that you were not to act like a servant but here you are, looking like a housemaid.'

'Mathilde is so busy,' Sarah protested. 'I can't sit around doing nothing when she's racing all over.'

She stood two steps from the bottom and looked at him with pleading eyes but he was not impressed.

'I have known her for most of my life and I do not recall seeing her race anywhere,' he countered irritably. 'If she is overworked I do not doubt that she will inform me. She is quite accustomed to making her opinions known, even in things that do not concern her. You will not assist with the work in the château, *mademoiselle*, and that is an order!'

Sarah stiffened with annoyance and she was just about to tell him what he could do with his orders when Violette walked through the open front door.

Seeing her here in the château brought a feeling of utter dismay to Sarah. Armand had brought Violette here because it was her right to be here and Sarah could see that, in spite of his momentary madness in feeling desire for her both at the apartment and in the stable, Violette was part of his life and almost certainly part of his future.

All the animation died from her face and she stood there irresolute, as if she had taken a blow.

'*Çà àlors!*' Violette burst into laughter and turned to Armand. 'So the secret is out, *chéri*? You have an English maid, *n'est-ce pas?*'

Sarah's face flushed with both annoyance and embarrassment. She was perfectly well aware of how she looked in jeans and a shirt, her hair covered with a scarf, and Violette was dressed to kill. She was also clearly capable of going for the jugular and Céline had been right: Violette did not like another female in the same house as Armand.

'Mademoiselle Thorpe has taken pity on Mathilde,' Armand said tightly, his eyes angrily on Sarah. 'She feels that Mathilde has too much to do.'

'But that is what she is paid for,' Violette said scornfully, looking at Sarah as if she were not too blessed with brainpower. 'It is necessary to be able to handle servants in a place like this château, *mademoiselle.*'

'I don't expect I'll be here long enough to learn,' Sarah said sharply, her blood beginning to boil. 'I'm more accustomed to handling books.'

'If there is anything I can do to help, *chéri*, then let me know,' Violette said, ignoring Sarah. 'I will do anything to get you to come back to Paris when I go next week. Shall I exercise the horses for you?'

'Mademoiselle Thorpe exercises the horses,' Armand stated, his eyes still fixed angrily on Sarah's face. 'They were seen to this morning.'

'But really!' Violette exclaimed, glancing at Sarah's slender figure. 'What a risk you are taking, Armand.'

'She is an expert!' Armand informed her in a caustic voice. 'She is better than both you and I together when it comes to handling horses.'

'And how do you know that I exercised them today?' Sarah suddenly asked angrily, tired of being spoken of as if she were not there at all. 'After all, I'm terribly busy myself, being a servant. Maybe I gave them a miss this morning?'

'You did not,' Armand replied, some of his anger fading to mockery. 'I watched you, *mademoiselle*. I watched you until you came back to the stables.'

'I would have thought you had better things to do with your time,' Sarah snapped. Violette was being ignored in this private battle and her eyes went from one to the other in annoyance but she said nothing.

'I do have other things to do with my time,' Armand agreed, his eyes filling with mocking amusement. 'They are not necessarily better things, however. Watching you is something I would not miss for the world.'

'Well, if she is so good, perhaps she should continue to exercise the animals,' Violette intervened sharply. 'You promised me coffee, *chéri*.'

'Of course I did,' Armand assured her smoothly. 'You will join us, *mademoiselle*?' His eyes came back to Sarah and she shook her head, carefully avoiding looking at him.

'I've had coffee with Mathilde, thank you,' she muttered. 'There's some on the stove.'

'Then we will get it for ourselves,' Armand said comfortably. 'You have finished your—cleaning?'

'For now!' Sarah glared at him, making it quite clear that she would do exactly as she liked. She did not like it, however, when she had to go into the kitchen and put away her equipment while Armand stared at her intently and Violette walked around as if she owned the place. She just wished Céline had been there to call this woman to order.

'Where is Madame Couvier?' Violette wanted to know when it became apparent that Céline was not going to make an appearance. Sarah was just bending down to the cupboard and she went very still, wondering how Armand was going to get out of that one. It served him right. Now he too could be embarrassed.

He was not embarrassed at all.

'Oh, she is away for a few days,' he said easily. 'My aunt is ill and naturally my mother had to go to her.'

'But. . . ?' Violette sounded shocked and Sarah decided that she could not stay in the cupboard any longer. She straightened up from her crouching position, her face flushing brightly when she found Armand's eyes running slowly over her slender flanks with very appreciative masculine speculation.

'We are managing,' Armand assured Violette smoothly, his eyes now on Sarah's rounded breasts. 'Mathilde is cooking and, as you can see, Sarah is helping.' It was one of the first times he had called her Sarah and Violette stiffened with annoyance. Sarah fled, her face flushing even more as Armand's eyes followed her progress with sardonic amusement.

She decided to stay in her room until they had gone and when Violette left Armand went with her. He would be having lunch with Violette and it made Sarah terribly miserable. The morning dragged on endlessly. Céline had phoned and Sarah told her cheerfully that everything was all right. It was not all right, though, because with Céline away there was nothing at all to take her mind from Armand.

She was not the same person who had come to the château and she knew that she would never be that person again. It had been a bitter-sweet experience and it was not by any means over. As far as seeing Armand was concerned, though, it was almost over. Soon he would be gone and she knew that when he left the light would go out of everything.

Sarah went for a walk and she was walking along a path beside the park when she heard the sound of a tractor and, looking up, she saw it across the nearest field. As the tractor turned, she saw that Armand was driving and it suddenly became urgent that he should not see her.

He had confessed, even in front of Violette, that he had watched her again this morning but she had not forgotten his other words—that she invited his attention by watching him. She had no intention of being caught doing that now and she turned quickly, not really looking where she was going.

There was a searing pain in her arm and Sarah spun away from it, only to find her hair caught and held fast at the top of the fence. Looking down, she saw blood trickling to her wrist and it was only then that she became aware that the fence was reinforced by barbed wire. It had cut deeply into her arm, caught her hair as she tried to escape and a slight pain by the side of her neck told her that she was scratched there too.

It was the arm, though, that had suffered most. She had not bothered with a jacket and the wire had cut deeply through her sweater and into the skin, with nothing to stop it. Sarah struggled to get her hair free, trying to detach the strands from the clinging wire, aware all the time that blood was soaking into her sweater.

'Sarah! *Mon Dieu*, what have you done to yourself?'
Armand was there, climbing the fence and leaping down
beside her. 'Hush! Keep still,' he ordered when she tried
to explain and tried to get her hair free.

Very gently, he disentangled her hair and then he
turned her towards him, his eyes on her arm. He said
nothing as he carefully rolled up her sleeve and by now
the pain was quite bad, making her feel sick.

'It—it's not as bad as it looks,' she managed faintly
but he shook his head, glancing at her white face.

'It is probably worse than it looks,' he muttered, taking
her gently by her other arm. 'Come, we will cut across
the park. I must get you back quickly.'

'What about the tractor?' she asked worriedly but
Armand's opinion of the tractor and its fate was short
and to the point. The French words she did not know
but the meaning was clear. The tractor was doomed to
a terrible fate in some fiery, underground world.

Mathilde was not there as they came into the kitchen
and Armand put Sarah into a chair by the fire and then
brought water and a cloth to bathe her arm. He knelt
down by her, every one of his actions careful, his hands
gentle on her skin.

'What were you doing to get yourself caught up on
the fence?' he asked with his usual impatience. 'You are
not careless.'

'I—I never noticed the wire and I turned a bit too
quickly.' She said nothing else but he glanced up at her
pale face.

'Because you saw me,' he growled. 'You did not want
me to think that you were following me around.'

'I wasn't!' Sarah protested loudly and then winced as
the water stung her arm.

'I'm sorry,' Armand said quietly. 'This must be
cleaned, though.' He looked at it carefully. 'It may
need stitching.'

'No!' Sarah regarded him with horror and he grimaced and then looked up at her wryly.

'I am not proposing to do it myself. My sewing skills are limited. De Brise will do it and you will also need an injection.'

'If you mean an anti-tetanus, I'm up to date,' Sarah said quickly. She didn't fancy any stitches and she looked even paler now.

Armand put the bowl down and then moved her hair aside, his eyes on her neck.

'You are scratched, too,' he murmured abruptly. 'It is lucky that the deeper cut is on your arm. On the softer skin of your neck it would have been more painful.'

'Thank you. It's painful enough where it is,' Sarah muttered shakily and his eyes met hers as he stood up, his glance edging on anger.

'You were like a cat in a net, struggling wildly. I thought you would be hurt much worse than this before I could get to you. It would have been better to allow me to think whatever I chose about your walk instead of attempting to prove that you were not guilty of watching me.'

'I *wasn't* watching you,' Sarah protested, quite sure of her ground because she had never expected even to see him.

'But you were afraid that I would think you were. We have a problem, you and I,' he finished quietly.

Once again, his eyes met hers and Sarah's tongue ran anxiously along her lips.

'I don't feel as if I've got a problem, apart from the accident I've had because you choose to use barbed wire on fences. My other problem is how to survive having this arm stitched. I'm not very brave.'

'No. I noticed,' he said sceptically. 'You take a high fence on horseback without a qualm yet you run from a spider. Now you fear a small amount of stitching. I would say that your courage is probably limited to horses.'

'Don't forget that I'm scared of storms and dark places,' Sarah snapped, glaring at him, and he smiled down at her with amused irony.

'I have not forgotten.' He suddenly softened and took pity on her. 'Come,' he said quietly. 'I will get you to De Brise and he can deal with that arm. It would also be a good idea to escape before Mathilde appears and tries her expertise on you.'

'Can't the cut just be left to get better by itself?' Sarah pleaded, but he drew her to her feet and firmly turned her to the door.'

'No, it cannot. There is nothing to fear because if he hurts you I will be there.'

'A fat lot of good that will do me,' Sarah pointed out crossly.

'I will intervene,' Armand promised in his normal ironic way. 'He is a little too old to be physically attacked but I will shout at him loudly and intimidate him.'

'Will the shouting include Violette?' Sarah enquired quite petulantly and he gave one of his low laughs as he led her to the Land Rover.

'It will not. Violette is not the doctor. She will merely be an interested bystander.'

'Don't you mean a gleeful bystander?' Sarah asked glumly as Armand watched her get into the vehicle.

'Perhaps,' he murmured, smiling at her sardonically. 'We will observe her, *n'est-ce pas*? At dinner tonight, we will compare notes on her attitude.'

As it turned out, Sarah need not have worried about stitches. Eric De Brise examined her arm, checked that she was up to date with her injections and then said that stitches would not be necessary. He was a little patronising.

'Nowadays, *mademoiselle*,' he informed her in an amused voice, 'we do not always need to stitch. There is this clever little white tape that serves very well.'

Sarah compressed her lips and managed to keep silent. She knew all about the clever little white tape. It was not the first time she had been cut. It did not improve matters that Violette stood there with a superior look on her face, either. Armand had not left Sarah's side and watched everything carefully but Violette had not been invited to the spectacle and Sarah was quietly simmering.

When the doctor left them for a minute, Armand glanced down at Sarah.

'You are all right?' he asked. It made her feel like a child who had to be taken care of and she almost snapped at him.

'Perfectly all right,' she assured him rather ungraciously. 'I'm not about to faint from a small cut.'

'It is not exactly small,' Armand reminded her, his dark eyes narrowing at her tone. Their glances locked and the anger drained from Sarah's face. She was allowing her annoyance with Violette to colour her attitude to Armand. He was looking after her. He was always looking after her and sometimes he was quite gentle. She looked up at him regretfully and he went on staring at her as if he was trying to read her mind.

'How did you come to get this cut?' Violette wanted to know, her eyes going from one to the other angrily.

'She did not notice the barbed wire. I will have to take it down from that particular fence. Obviously it is dangerous.'

It gave Sarah a warm feeling that he was covering up for her and she looked up at him again with a grateful expression on her face, managing a slight smile as his eyes met hers. It looked a little conspiratorial and Violette clearly thought that too.

'Mademoiselle Thorpe can stay with us,' she offered sharply. 'I will mention it to my father. There is plenty of room in this house.'

'She is not in need of constant medical attention,' Armand pointed out coldly. 'This was an accident. Normally she is capable of taking care of herself.' Sarah knew that this was a debatable point. She was not capable of taking care of herself with Armand, and was barely capable with Craig, but Armand's intervention had at least settled her heart's leap of alarm. There was no way she wanted to be anywhere near to Violette De Brise and going back to England had immediately sprung to her mind.

'I wasn't thinking of medical treatment,' Violette answered irritably. 'It is a matter of propriety.'

'Really?' Armand's voice was dangerously ironic but Violette was either quite accustomed to getting her own way or too incensed to notice.

'With Madame Couvier away, you are alone in the château,' she insisted with growing annoyance. 'It is not exactly proper.'

'I am perfectly safe, *ma chère*,' Armand murmured sarcastically. 'When it was foggy, Sarah stayed with me at my apartment in Paris and never once attacked me. She has not attacked me at the château either. I do not even lock my door.'

Sarah felt her face flushing. She was well aware that she was listening to a private battle that was about to become more caustic any second and she was astounded that he was prepared to react like this with Violette.

'The whole village will be talking!' Violette spat, her face red with anger.

Armand's next words were delivered in French. Calmly and succinctly, with no outward display of annoyance, he condemned the village to the same fate as the tractor. It silenced Violette and left Sarah awestricken.

CHAPTER NINE

SARAH still felt like that on the way back and Armand said nothing at all. From his expression it could have been supposed that no cross word had been spoken. Sarah sat quietly and chewed at her lip. She could not quite understand his attitude although she knew he was not a man to be ordered about and Violette had certainly tried that.

'Er—about the village,' she began hesitantly and Armand never looked across at her.

'You wish to move out of the château? You are worried about your reputation?' he asked coolly.

'I am not!' Sarah said sharply. 'I never even thought of it and I didn't want to move out.'

'Then we will not argue,' he suggested quietly.

'But Violette...'

'Does not control my activities,' he finished for her flatly. 'Violette needs to be reined in from time to time.'

'There was no need to tell her about—about Paris,' Sarah murmured and he gave a hard laugh.

'Why not? In any case, she would have been told by that idiot Georges the next time she came to the apartment.'

'Does she go there?' Sarah asked quietly. 'I mean, does she...?'

'Sleep at the apartment, *mademoiselle*. She is a grown woman, after all, and in charge of her own destiny.'

Sarah felt as if she had been savagely put down and she relapsed into silence. He could not have stated more

148

plainly that Violette slept with him; no wonder she was incensed about this arrangement at the château.

'So, what have you decided?' Armand asked when it became quite clear that Sarah was not going to speak again. 'If you are content to stay as we are until Céline returns, I can see no problem.'

'Of course I'm content to stay,' Sarah muttered, turning her face away. 'I promised your mother and I'm sure she will be back quickly.'

'The speed of her return will depend on how much she wants to be with you and how far she dares go in ignoring Martine's attack. Normally, I would say that you would win easily but I can almost guarantee that Céline will have made a tactical error. She will have told Martine about you. There is a lot of mileage in that, *mademoiselle*. Martine will find it fascinating and her illness will be correspondingly longer.'

'I can't see why she would think it fascinating,' Sarah grumbled.

'You cannot?' he inquired drily. 'You underestimate yourself, *ma chère*. You fascinate all of us.'

Sarah was silent. At the moment they were both wary of each other but underneath it all the feelings were still smouldering. Even the way that Armand spoke to her told her that. It would be a very good thing when Céline returned but then, no doubt, Armand would go. It was all impossible and she sighed shakily. So much of her time was spent in thinking about Armand.

'What is it? You are all right?' he asked quickly, his derisive tone dying away, and Sarah nodded, giving him a brief smile.

'Yes. It's just that—that things are so complicated.'

He stopped the Land Rover at the steps of the château and looked across at her with dark, probing eyes.

'Emotions are always complicated,' he assured her softly, a half-smile on his face. 'It takes time to grow into them. There has not been time.'

Sarah just looked at him, knowing quite well what he was saying and wondering if he was meaning her own emotions or his. Armand's gaze roamed over her face and his smile was rather rueful.

'When I knew about you,' he said quietly, 'I was quite prepared to meet a girl who had been allowed too much liberty—a spoiled little rich girl, very well-versed in the ways of the world. But I was wrong. You have been sheltered in many ways and there are gaps in your knowledge that have never been filled.'

'You're saying that I'm like a child?' Sarah accused him and he laughed, tilting her face to the light.

'Oh, no. You are certainly not that. You are just a peculiar mixture, and I confess to being cautious about you. I am not sure whether I should guard you with my life or make love to you.'

Sarah gasped and looked at him with wide, astounded eyes, her cheeks flushing softly.

'I suppose you think you can get away with statements like that because you're French?' she asked shakily. 'People don't—don't speak to me like that.'

'The *person* I saw with you was not speaking,' Armand reminded her darkly, his smile dying away. 'He was treating you badly. Later, it occurred to me that you submitted because you had no idea how to cope with him. That being the case, I have decided to guard you. I will explain this to Violette and she will understand and be easier in her mind.'

Sarah didn't know whether he was mocking her or being serious and she looked at him anxiously.

'Please, Armand! I don't want her to know anything about me.'

His eyes roamed again over her face, resting on her lips, his smile very much one of mockery.

'She already knows all that interests her,' he murmured. 'She knows that you are beautiful and that I am not willing to hand you over to her care. She does not know quite what you mean to my mother and I am not about to tell her. I do not gossip. Violette will have to live with her jealousy until this is all over. Come. Mathilde will wish to know about your adventure.'

He came round to help her out and Sarah could not look at him; she was too miserable. He had stated quite clearly that when she went he would make it up to Violette and the thought bit into her savagely. Violette was not the only one to be jealous; Sarah was jealous herself because she wanted Armand to be more than just kind to her. She wanted him to stake some sort of claim on her and it was impossible. He already had a life that did not include her.

The next morning, when Sarah came downstairs, Armand was in the kitchen preparing breakfast and she stood in the doorway and looked at him in astonishment.

'What are you doing? Where is Mathilde?'

'It is her day off,' he muttered. 'I had forgotten. We are left helpless to manage as best we can. I am managing breakfast, as you see.'

'Well, I'm not helpless,' Sarah assured him, coming in briskly and taking things out of his hands without any hesitation. 'I'm quite capable of making breakfast, lunch and dinner.'

'Ah! I fear that you are about to be disappointed.' Armand sat down and watched her with an amused smile on his face. 'Mathilde left a note on the table. A cold lunch is in the fridge and she is willing to come in and cook dinner; in fact, she insists. It is because of your fragility and your accident.'

'I'm a good cook!' Sarah snapped, looking at him with stormy eyes. It only amused him further.

'Do not be angry with me, *petite*,' he begged softly. 'I would love to watch you make dinner and, as it happens, I enjoy English cooking. However, I think we should fit in with Mathilde's plans for today. If we anger her she may take reprisals. If she does, I will shout at her, she will resign and Céline will come back to turmoil.'

'That seems to be a very complicated way to get out of eating my cooking,' Sarah muttered, getting on with making coffee. 'Why don't you simply say that you prefer Mathilde to cook?'

'Because I do not,' he assured her quietly. 'If you were cooking the dinner I would come back early to watch you.' Sarah went silent, not knowing if he was joking. There was no smile on his face, though, and she sat down with her meal, uncertain what to say. Armand ate his breakfast in silence too, and it was only as he was finishing his coffee that he looked at her.

'Let me see your arm,' he ordered, standing and coming round to her side.

'It's all right,' Sarah said hastily but Armand was not usually put off when his mind was made up.

'I will decide,' he stated grimly. As he unwound the bandage and carefully inspected her arm, Sarah tried to still her trembling but it was a hard battle and as he glanced at her quickly she knew she had not won. He knew she was trembling and he also knew why. The kitchen suddenly seemed terribly quiet.

The white tape was still in place with no sign of any redness outside it and Armand steadily re-bandaged the arm and then stood looking down at her.

'If Céline does not come back soon, I think you should go home for a while,' he said quietly.

'Why?' The distress in Sarah's eyes was very clear and his face darkened.

'You know why, Sarah. You know also that this cannot go on indefinitely.' He trailed one brown finger gently down her cheek. 'Perhaps you can hide around corners for a very long time. I cannot.' She looked up at him and his eyes held her fast. 'I want you,' he said softly, 'and it is not going to magically go away. It will only grow.'

He turned and walked out of the back door that led to the courtyard and Sarah was still sitting there in a daze when she heard the Land Rover drive past the front of the château. She now had no choice at all. Very quietly and very gently, Armand had asked her to leave. She would have to break her word to her father, make an excuse to Céline and then come back when Armand was not there.

She stood and began to clear the kitchen. For now she would carry on as usual but at lunchtime, if Armand came in, she would bring up the subject and make arrangements. There was no getting out of it, although she felt on the edge of tears. Armand wanted her to go and she could not refuse. It was, after all, the best thing to do.

Just before lunchtime Sarah heard a car stop outside the château. It was not the Land Rover and for a moment her heart lifted at the thought that it might be Céline. She went to the window to look and a great stab of panic hit her when she saw that, far from being Céline, it was Craig. He was standing outside the car, looking at the château with interest, and Sarah seemed to be frozen to the spot.

It was impossible but he was there, looking inordinately pleased with himself and very determined. There was a set look to his mouth that she knew all too well. Somehow he had found her and he had come to take her back. Even though she now had to go, she would not leave with Craig. All her efforts to be free of him would be defeated if she simply left with him now.

Her next thought brought back the panic rapidly. It was almost time for lunch. Armand would be returning and there would be trouble of a kind that she could scarcely imagine. She raced into the hall and flew down the steps with no further thought than to get Craig away from here at once.

Craig obviously thought her greeting was indicative of her state of mind. She had just appeared and raced towards him and he came round the car with a satisfied look on his face.

'Sarah, love! I knew you needed me. I've been to a hell of a lot of trouble to find you but it's all worthwhile now I know you're so glad.'

She just ignored his words, evading him when he reached out for her.

'Craig! You must be mad to come here! How did you find me?' His smile died at her agitated words, a hard look coming into his eyes.

'Easy, my pet,' he jeered. 'You mentioned a village— St Clair. You also mentioned a château. It was a matter of maps and questions. I found you with very little difficulty. Everybody in that village knows you live here.'

'I asked you not to come,' Sarah reminded him. She stood looking at him in a flurry of anxiety and he smiled at her as if she was simply playing hard to get.

'You know I want you back,' he explained carefully, walking towards her. 'It's hellish without you. Why keep this up, Sarah? Finally you'll see some sense and come home. Do it now and I'll take you away this minute.'

'I am not coming back!' Sarah snapped. 'I've told you that and you have no reason to expect that I even miss you. Coming here without an invitation is just unforgivable.'

'I don't intend to go inside,' he snapped. 'I came to get you. Now stop this damned nonsense and collect your things.'

It was like banging her head against a wall. Nothing she said seemed to make any impression on him and Sarah was aware all the time that at any moment Armand might drive up to the château.

'Please leave, Craig,' she managed quietly. 'I made a promise and I'm sticking to it.'

'I'll deal with the promise,' he asserted with growing anger. 'Where is this woman you're with? I'll explain to her.'

'There's nothing to explain!' Sarah informed him furiously, forgetting her anxiety in her utter astonishment that he thought he could behave like this. 'Céline is away, as it happens. She might not be back for days. If you hang around here for much longer, Armand is going to appear and he's not going to be pleased.'

She knew she had said the wrong thing when his face tightened and he reached out quickly and caught her arm. It was exactly where she had injured herself and Sarah gave a cry of pain that he ignored completely. He tightened his grip, dragging her forward as she tried desperately to get her arm free.

'So who is staying in this place?' he snarled. 'You, the saintly Armand and who else?'

'Nobody else, *monsieur*, and I am not at all saintly!' The dark, savage voice cut through the quiet morning like the slash of a steel blade and both of them turned to see Armand almost upon them. He had come from the courtyard and Sarah looked at him with desperate eyes, begging for rescue. 'Go inside, Sarah!' Armand ordered harshly. 'I will see your guest off the premises.'

'Not without her!' Craig tightened his grip, making Sarah cry out again, and Armand looked at him with dark, icy eyes.

'Let her go or I will break your arm,' he ordered in a frighteningly reasonable voice and Craig let her go immediately. Sarah stood there clutching her arm. Her face was white, she was shaking from head to foot and when those icy eyes turned back to her she just fled, stumbling up the flight of steps to the door and running into the kitchen.

She was ashamed, embarrassed and her arm hurt so badly that she wanted to cry. She heard the car leave and braced herself for the onslaught of rage she knew she would have to face. She had never seen Armand so angry, and she stood facing the door, waiting for him to come.

He walked in and looked at her with cold fury on his face. He came no further than the doorway of the kitchen, seemingly unsure of his ability to control his temper.

'It is normally considered to be polite to inform your host when you intend to invite a guest to the house, *mademoiselle*,' he rasped. 'Fortunately, the château is isolated, so we do not have to give explanations to interested neighbours.'

'I didn't invite him,' Sarah protested in a trembling voice. 'I didn't even tell him where I was.'

Armand gave her a coldly sceptical look.

'He consulted a clairvoyant? Do not insult my intelligence!'

'He knew I was staying in a château and—and I accidentally told him the name of the village and...'

'Accidentally?' he queried with acid sarcasm. 'What a misfortune!' He took two steps forward, his face dark with anger. 'I warned you not to insult my intelligence. You cannot manage without him? Just say so and I will get out the car and catch him up. If your need for him is so urgent I will even have your clothes sent on!'

'I've *told* you!' Sarah said bitterly. 'I didn't want to see him. He was determined to find me and get me to go back. You must have seen how he was treating me and yet you still——'

'I note that once again you did not take the expert swing at him that you took at me.'

'He was hurting me.' Sarah bent her head, tears filling her eyes. It seemed that Armand was as violent as Craig, too obsessed with his pride to take any notice that she was hurting. 'He—he grabbed my arm right on the place where...'

She never had the chance to say more because Armand covered the ground between them with a few swift strides. Before she could even look up he had pulled her into his arms, his hand cradling her head against his shoulder.

'Don't cry, *ma petite*,' he urged softly. 'It is all right now. He has gone.'

'But you're still here,' Sarah choked, looking up at him miserably. 'You're angry and you think I invited him. You think I wanted to be with him.'

'I do not,' he said softly, pulling her head back to his shoulder. 'You have just been listening to a combination of rage and jealousy.' She went very still and he lifted her face, cupping it in his hands. 'Oh, yes,' he confessed roughly, 'I am jealous. I was so jealous that I did not even realise he had a grip on your injured arm.' He moved her to the table and gently pushed her into a chair. 'Let me see,' he ordered. 'And do not tell me that it is all right.'

Armand swore softly under his breath when he saw the red marks of the tight grip that had been used to pull her forward. The tape was still in place but her arm was slightly swollen.

'We had better see De Brise,' he said tightly but Sarah was adamant.

'No! He'll want to know about the fingermarks. I—I don't feel like facing an interrogation.'

'The wound may have opened,' Armand reminded her. He was bandaging it up but he still looked determined and Sarah insisted.

'I'll chance it. If it's bad tomorrow I'll see somebody.'

'Somebody?' He looked at her quickly and Sarah sighed and dropped her gaze.

'You've got a very short memory for such an intelligent man. At breakfast-time, you asked me to leave.'

'And you intend to?' His hand tilted her face, forcing her to look at him. 'Your transport has just gone. By now he will be through the village and on to the main road.'

'Oh, don't!' Sarah begged quietly. 'I'm not going to Craig. I don't want to see him ever again. I'm just going home.'

'You are not,' he stated firmly, pulling her into his arms. 'He tried to take you away but I would have killed him rather than let you go.'

'You—you said...' Sarah stared up at him with hope in her eyes, her whole body waiting.

'I wanted to protect you,' Armand said quietly. 'It occurs to me that I can protect you best right here.' He held her slightly away and looked at her seriously. 'We will just stay out of each other's way, hmm? Soon Céline will be home; in fact, she will be home immediately if I inform her that you are injured.'

'Oh, don't do that,' Sarah begged thoughtlessly and he looked down into her face, his eyes moving slowly along the trembling line of her lips.

'I will pretend that your plea was compassion for Céline,' he murmured. For a second his head bent towards her, his firm lips softening, and then he snapped his head back, his arms falling to his sides. 'Let us have this lunch that Mathilde prepared,' he ordered. 'I am here so I may as well eat.'

'I'll get it,' Sarah offered shakily but she was once again firmly placed in a chair.

'I will get it. First I will make you a cup of tea. I am sure that of the two of us I am in the better condition.'

'I never took the horses out today,' Sarah confessed, anxious to sound normal and bright.

'And do not dare,' Armand ordered sharply, glancing across at her with dark, flashing eyes. 'Today and tomorrow at least you will not ride at all. I will get the two long-suffering men to do the job. The horses will be disappointed but they must learn that life has its more sombre moments. The men dare not take the hedge at all. They consider you to be some sort of circus act. They are duly impressed.'

'Do they watch me too?' Sarah asked shakily, looking down at her hands as Armand presented her with her tea. He smiled that wry smile, his eyes on her fair head.

'Apparently. They are watching you for entirely different reasons, however. For myself, I hardly see the horses.'

Céline phoned after dinner and while she was talking to Armand Sarah disappeared to bed. Her arm was hurting her and she felt quite dispirited. She had expected her stay here to be a problem, even before she had left England, but she had never envisaged the problem it had become.

There was no doubt about her feelings for Armand and she knew that if she deliberately set out to encourage him his iron will would probably snap. She didn't want that at all; in fact she had no idea what she wanted, except that she dreaded going and never seeing him again.

She lay for a long time staring into the darkness. Her arm was just too uncomfortable to make going to sleep easy and her mind was in too much of a turmoil to help. Twice, Armand had come to her rescue with Violette, taking her side against the woman he was obviously close to. Now he had openly confessed to jealousy, his rage at Craig's appearance leaving her in no doubt about it.

But he had wanted her to go and deep down she knew he would breathe a sigh of relief when she left the château. Nothing made sense. The only steadfast thing was her father's desire to send her to Céline and heal both of them. Tears came to her eyes when she thought of it. His very last act had been to try and make them both happy. He could never have anticipated that she would...would...

Sarah stared into the darkened room. Love Armand? Was that what it was? A shiver ran over her skin, brought on by a feeling of happiness and anguish. Had love crept up on her like this? Her reaction to him from the first had been deep and now she just wanted to see him all the time, be with him all the time, even when he was angry. She wanted his arms around her, wanted his kisses.

She got out of bed, putting the light on and pacing the room. She had disposed of the problem of Craig but now she had a problem that would not go away. Love did not go away. It was more imperative than ever that she leave here, but she knew that she did not want to go. She needed to be with Armand.

Her arm was throbbing and she held it against her. There was nothing here for her to take and she had no idea where Céline kept things like aspirin. If anywhere, they would most likely be in the place where Céline spent so much of her time—the kitchen. She put on her robe and tightened it around her slim waist. Even if there was nothing down there to ease the pain, at least she could make herself a hot drink.

The château was silent but now it did not intimidate her. The lights were on when she stepped into the passage and she went down the long stairs quite quickly. It was a little chilly by now but she knew that the kitchen was warm and cosy.

As her feet left the carpet and stepped on to the flagged floor of the hall she looked down in surprise, pulling a wry face when she realised that she had forgotten to put on her slippers. It proved how bemused she was but she hesitated to go back for them. She walked quickly to the kitchen and switched on the lights, pleased to find that the room was still very warm.

None of the cupboards helped in her search for pain-killers. Some of the labels she knew, but the ones she could not understand had to be left strictly alone and Sarah waited for the kettle to boil, sitting by the dying fire in one of the big chairs. The fancy china clock told her that it was midnight and the silence of the place would normally have worried her. As it was, she had too much to think about, too many other things to worry her without being timid about the quiet of the château——

A noise just outside the back door had her spinning round and then jumping to her feet and she was standing like that, her eyes wide with fright, when Armand walked in.

'I thought you were asleep!' Sarah exclaimed accusingly and his own eyes widened, his dark brows lifting in surprise.

'Meaning that you only creep around when I am dead to the world?' he enquired. He stood exactly where he was, staring at her for a second, and then he turned, closing and locking the door.

'I—I didn't know I was by myself upstairs,' Sarah pointed out. 'I thought you were asleep so I...'

'You were not by yourself for very long. The horses were disturbed. From my room I can hear them. I went to have a look but they are all right. It was, perhaps, a fox.'

The kettle began to boil and Sarah glanced at it, not sure now what to do.

'You came to make a drink?' Armand looked at her steadily. 'Would you like me to make it?'

'No! No, I—I'll make it. Do you want one?' She knew she was avoiding his eyes but she didn't dare to look at him and Armand moved impatiently.

'I would like a drink if I can be certain that my presence does not drive you to terror!' His voice rasped out at her and Sarah looked at him quickly, biting at her lip, her anxiety very obvious.

'You startled me when you came in. I came down for a cup of tea and to see if I could find an aspirin or something.'

'The arm is hurting?' He strode over to her, his anger gone but a deep frown on his face. 'Let me look.'

'There's really nothing... It's just throbbing and...'

'Sarah!' he grated as she almost shrank from him. 'I am not about to attack you. Let me look.' When she reluctantly held out her arm he held her wrist and gently felt around the wound and Sarah's eyes were drawn to his strong hands, to the almost tender way they held her. It would be heavenly to be held like that in his arms; her cheeks flushed even more and she bit at her lip as she felt trembling start deep inside her.

'It is not too swollen,' he murmured. 'Tomorrow we will keep a close eye on it and if the pain is bad we will go back to see De Brise. By then, the red marks will have gone and you will not be embarrassed.'

He looked up and Sarah quickly looked away, her heart fluttering.

'Thank you. I'll make my tea. Do you want tea?'

'Coffee. I will find some aspirin for you. Céline usually keeps things like that in the top cupboard. She appears to think that no one is to be trusted with pain-killers.'

Sarah knew he was talking to ease away the strain between them and she was grateful, but nothing would stop her trembling now; it was growing. The hand that held the kettle was none too steady and she spilled water, not managing to jump back quickly enough as it splashed on the floor.

'*Ciel*! Now what?' Armand growled, springing forward and taking her shoulders in a hard grip. He sat her in the chair again and before she could stop him he was kneeling with her foot in his hand as he inspected it for any burns.

'It's nothing,' she said unevenly. 'I almost got out of the way.'

'In the same way that you almost did not cut yourself on the barbed wire!' he muttered. 'I am beginning to be anxious if you are out of my sight.'

One hand was gently massaging her foot, the other was on her ankle, and Sarah felt everything inside her begin to melt. His hands were sensuous on her skin, touching her like a lover, and as his fingers slid to her calf he lifted her foot, bending his head to kiss her toes gently.

A little whimper of sound left Sarah's trembling lips and Armand looked up at her with dark, burning eyes. For a moment they stayed like that, emotion flaring between them, sensation like stars in the air, sparkling, electrical, as if the whole room was a bewitching world and they were at the centre of it.

Irresistibly, Sarah was drawn to him, her eyes on his dark face as she leaned forward, and he stood in one lithe movement, pulling her to her feet and into his arms.

'Oh, Sarah!' he whispered hoarsely. 'What is madness after all—keeping you or letting you go?'

His lips searched urgently for hers and Sarah clung to him, her arms tightly around his neck, her body soft against his hard strength.

'You want this, *chérie*?' he asked huskily. 'You want to be in my arms?'

'Oh, yes!' He could have no doubt about her answer because, as his body hardened demandingly against hers, she came to him with alluring softness.

'I want to make love to you,' he warned thickly but this time he received no answer except the enticing moan of need that left her lips and the bewitching sweetness of the silkily pliant body in his arms.

Sarah was barely aware of it when Armand lifted her. The strong arms were so familiar, the kisses being rained on her face and neck so perfect, so right, that the journey through the hall and along the passage upstairs was dream-like. It was only when she felt the softness of a bed beneath her that she opened her eyes. It was an unfamiliar bed, a room she had never ventured into, and Armand leaned over her, looking down into her eyes.

'My bed, *chérie*,' he said unevenly. 'You must decide now if you want to stay with me.'

She never answered but the slender arms that reached for him said all he wished to know and, with a low groan of pleasure, he came down beside her, turning her into his arms, holding her close.

'Beautiful Sarah,' he whispered against her skin. 'Don't be afraid of me. There is just you and me and we will forget everything else tonight.'

No thought of fear was in her mind; nothing mattered but Armand. He was a strong, dark being who held her close and murmured words she could not understand but they were words that echoed inside her, husky protestations of need, whispered words of passion, and once again her skin burned, and her body moved softly with every unspoken command.

Sarah's hand came to touch his face but he took her hand in his, turning it to his lips, his tongue tracing exotic patterns on her palm. He drew her fingers into his mouth, sucking them one by one until Sarah felt a deep burst of flame inside her and moved urgently against him. He drew her hand to his chest, inviting her touch, and beneath the parted buttons his skin was taut, every muscle tense, waiting.

Armand shuddered as she opened more buttons and spread her hand on his chest, her fingers curling in the crisp, dark, masculine hair, and his shuddering enjoyment gave her courage to continue, to slide her hand further inside and stroke along the smooth strength of his shoulder and then curve around his nape, invitingly tugging him towards her.

He gasped her name when her fingers shakily tried to unfasten his shirt more. She wanted to feel him closer, wanted it so much that there was desperation in her movements and he felt it.

'Let me do that,' he ordered unevenly, tearing open the shirt and tossing it aside. 'And let me do what I have wanted to do for so long. Let me look at you, *chérie*, let me touch you.'

Sarah's nightie and robe seemed to simply drift away, following the rest of Armand's clothes to the floor, and for a moment he looked down at her, his eyes blazing as they moved over her body. He looked into her eyes for one blinding second and then she was caught close, her mouth captured in a kiss so stingingly sweet that Sarah felt as if her heart would burst with joy.

'I'm aware of you every second, even when you are not there, close to me,' he whispered. 'And when I see you, I ache for you.'

His hand cupped her breast and then his head bent as he took the swollen nipple into his mouth. Sarah cried out sharply, fierce waves of pleasure shooting over her as he pulled her closer. She began to tremble uncontrollably and Armand relented, his hand warm and comforting, covering the sweet, stinging pain as his lips sought hers again. Her lips opened wide beneath his, welcoming the sensuous questing of his tongue, and his grip on her became demanding, urgent.

She was inexperienced but her whole being was on fire; little cries forced themselves from her lips at the strong caressing of his hands, the devouring passion of his mouth and she arched against him, seeking his body like an instinct to survive. Her fingers slid down his hips, her nails trailing across his skin, and the hands that caressed her tightened almost to pain as she wound her slender legs around his.

'Now, Sarah! It must be now,' he gasped as he drew her beneath him and Sarah's world rocked with pain and pleasure as he possessed her hungrily.

He stopped as he felt her pain, his hand stroking her face, but as the moment passed only the unearthly pleasure was left, the astounding joy of feeling Armand inside her, the heady knowledge that she was now not one person alone. She was closer to him than she had been to anyone. He was part of her. Love seared through her and she moved against him, her body welcoming him even more, every defence gone. Her arms wrapped round him and as he looked down at her she stared back with glowing, dreamy eyes.

'You love me!' he whispered, his eyes staring into hers. His face softened from the dark passion that had been there before. 'You love me, *chérie*!'

It was no question. It was a triumphant exclamation and he waited for no answer. As her eyes closed in submission, he moved inside her with exquisite gentleness, his mouth covering hers in an endless kiss that lasted until the universe danced around them and disappeared in exploding stars.

'Armand! Armand!' She came back to earth calling his name and his grip on her tightened, reassuring her until she opened her eyes. He was hovering over her, the dark gaze consuming her, his face tautly possessive. For a second they looked at each other raptly and then the burning eyes softened and a smile touched his lips.

'A virgin,' he murmured. 'In my desire to possess you, I forgot.'

'You didn't know,' Sarah whispered and his smile grew as his eyes moved over her flushed face.

'Then let us say that I assumed,' he suggested quietly. He stroked back her hair and when he looked at her again his glance was tender. 'You belong to me. Do you know that, *chérie*? You belong to me more than any woman has ever done before. At this moment I feel that I am the keeper of your soul.'

'That's frightening.' Sarah searched his face for some sign that he returned the love she had shown so clearly but he moved to the side of her, pulling her into his arms.

'Why should it frighten you?' he asked softly. 'I am strong enough to protect it, fierce enough to fight for it. It is safe with me and I do not intend to give it back.'

'Sometimes you say the strangest things,' Sarah complained as she snuggled against him and his arms closed even more tightly round her, his hands gently searching her silken skin. She felt laughter bubble through him and he bent his head to kiss her lingeringly.

'It is not something to worry about,' he assured her. 'You are safer than you have ever been, because you are part of me.'

Sarah was still puzzling over his words when she fell asleep. She had never even thought of moving, never considered going to her room, and the future was very far from her mind. She was another person. A miracle had happened to her in this silent château, and who could question a miracle?

CHAPTER TEN

THE phone beside Armand's bed was ringing, the shrill sound pulling Sarah back from a deep sleep, and she felt him stir against her. His arms left her as he leaned across to silence it.

'*Oui*?' he questioned briefly and then he was just listening for a long time. Sarah wound her arms round him, snuggling closer, and his free hand came to caress her although he never looked round. From time to time he grunted with annoyance and when he put the phone down and turned to face her his expression was one of rueful exasperation.

'It is the office,' he told her regretfully. 'I am needed there today.' When Sarah's eyes widened mournfully, he pulled himself upright, smiling down at her. 'If you recall, *chérie*, I said that sometimes it is easier to be there than to attempt any holiday.'

'You don't have a holiday,' Sarah reminded him. 'You work all the time.'

'You would like a holiday, hmm?' Armand lifted her into his arms, his lips teasing hers. 'I will be back to-night. If you tell me where you would like us to go, we will arrange it.'

'But I can't... What will Céline think? She doesn't know about...'

'She will know soon enough,' Armand pointed out, his hands beginning to make an exploration of her body. 'Who is Céline to disapprove? She must surely be the world's most faithful mistress.'

He pulled her close, his lips taking over from his searching hands, and Sarah melted against him, unable to resist, but inside the glowing warmth was wavering, a chill threatening the miracle. What had he meant? Did he intend to keep her as a mistress? Had Armand planned her fate like that? Last night he had been passionate, tender, and passion was growing in him now but the triumph in his eyes, the possession on his face had given no evidence of love.

'Oh, Sarah, Sarah! I don't want to leave you,' he murmured, sliding lower in bed and taking her with him. 'I want you in my arms all day.'

'What time is it?' Sarah stroked his face, her eyes unable to show anything but adoration and complete surrender and he grimaced at her reminder, his white teeth nipping her skin.

'It is eight. There is a meeting immediately after lunch and I have many papers to prepare before then. I will be back this evening but it is quite clear that I cannot stay here much longer.' He sat on the edge of the bed and turned to look at her. 'Promise or not, *ma petite*, we will have to move to Paris. Tonight I will gently break the news to Céline.'

He didn't ask what she thought. He strode off to the shower and Sarah hastily gathered her clothes, slipping into her robe. Armand was taking her with him, probably tomorrow, and he had said not one word about love. He had declared himself to be the keeper of her soul, had realised triumphantly that she loved him, but he had said nothing.

For a second, Sarah stood anxiously thinking, and then she hurried to her own room. Mathilde would be here soon and before then she must be much more prepared to face an inquisitive world. There was nothing she could do. She could not demand love. She could not even enquire. All she could do was wait. She went to shower and came back to find Armand just coming into her room; he was ready, dressed, light-hearted and smiling.

'Your arm, *ma chérie*?' he asked. 'I never thought of it when we woke up.'

Sarah blushed softly, her mind spinning back to waking in Armand's arms, and she looked quickly away from his dark, questioning eyes.

'It's fine, almost better. I took off the bandage.' She held her arm out, knowing that he would insist, and he came to inspect it.

'It looks good,' he pronounced, moulding her to him. 'You will take care today?' He tilted her face and Sarah nodded, her expression still anxious.

'It is all right, Sarah,' he said softly, looking into her eyes. 'I told you that it had happened too fast. I wanted things to go more gently. Circumstances drove all thought of restraint out of my mind, though, and you have not had time to get used to the emotion. I will teach you, *chérie*. I will take care of you until that bewildered look goes from your beautiful face. When I come back to-night we will have a long talk.'

He held her close, kissing her deeply, and then he was gone, leaving her trembling and more bemused than ever. She had no idea what she was to Armand but whatever she was she belonged to him and could never think of any sort of life without him.

He went without breakfast, his car pulling away even before she was dressed, and Sarah felt a colder quiet settle over the château and over her heart. She forced herself to relax, seeing a different person in the mirror when she inspected herself. It brought the smile back to her eyes, the warmth back to her skin. She loved Armand; she belonged to him. Nothing could go wrong.

Of course, she exercised the horses. She wanted to shout loudly that she loved Armand. There was nobody to tell but out in the cold sunlight, with a horse as a companion, she could re-live the whole wonderful night, the whole devastating feeling of love.

She was just riding back through the park, her cheeks flushed and her eyes shining, when she saw a car pulled up by the edge of the drive and her heart sank as she saw Violette watching her.

'You are very good,' Violette congratulated her. 'Better than good—you are brilliant. What a blessing that you have this skill.'

Sarah wanted to ride away. She did not want to face this woman and have her mind recognise that Violette had undoubtedly spent time at the apartment with Armand. She could not simply ignore her, though, and she reined in and looked down at the dark, attractive woman with eyes like ice.

'Thank you,' she said quietly. 'At least it means that I can make myself useful.'

'And pass the boring time away,' Violette finished for her. 'A whole month of imprisonment! How can you keep it up? How can anyone demand that of you? You must have been very devoted to your father, *mademoiselle.*'

'What do you mean?' Sarah stiffened, staring down into the upturned face. She had never mentioned her father to Violette and she was quite sure that Céline would not have done so either. Céline was discreet and in any case she did not like Violette.

'Oh, you know what I mean,' Violette assured her with a wry smile. 'When Armand told me that you were to be kept here for a month no matter how they managed it, I was speechless. It is like the Dark Ages. Madame Couvier must have been devoted to your father to agree to such a thing, as if you were a child still!'

'What are you talking about?' Sarah asked in a choked voice, a bitter chill coming to her skin. How could Violette know anything unless Armand had told her?

'According to Armand, you have become entangled with a man who did not meet with your father's approval. He wanted you here to get you out of the way. I would certainly not allow anyone to treat me like that, even if *madame* is a friend of your family.'

Sarah just stared at her and then turned the horse away.

'You are mistaken, Mademoiselle De Brise,' she said shortly. 'I am here to get to know Céline better. I believe I told you that in the village.'

'Well, it is not what Armand says and Armand and I are very close, as you no doubt know. He tells me that originally he objected to this plan but Madame Couvier talked him round after you came here. I am very understanding. I recognise the duty he has so I can spare him for a while but I feel so sorry for you, *mademoiselle*.'

Sarah rode away fast, the final words ringing in her ears. She dared not allow herself to think until she was safely in her room, and then it was all too miserably clear. Armand had said that her innocence was a burden and he had not meant just her lack of experience. It was her naïveté, her trust in people. She had trusted Céline, believed that her father had sent her here to recover from her loss. She had trusted her father, obeyed him without question. She had trusted Armand with her heart and all the time she was merely being kept away from London, from Craig.

Was that why Armand had been so angry about Craig? Was that why he had made love to her—because he had wanted her anyway and now he thought she was tied to France for a long time? Little wonder he had not spoken of love and little wonder that he had readily decided to take her to Paris when he came back. What did it matter where she was, providing she was not in London? Oh, Céline must have loved her father deeply to have agreed to this and, after meeting her, Armand must have been stunned at her naïveté in believing the story. She had simply swallowed everything without question—like an innocent fool.

Sarah's mind searched for another explanation, desperately clinging to Armand, but each time she thought it out she came back to the same conclusion. Violette knew, and who could have told her if it was not Armand? And why should Armand tell her such a tale unless it were true? He had said that he would placate Violette later and that alone meant that he would be seeing her and making it up after Sarah had gone. He had not waited to do that. He had told her when he'd gone to dinner with Violette and her father, no doubt finding time to be alone with her. Violette's father would expect them to wish to be alone. His manner at the café had shown that he knew all about them.

Now it was impossible to stay. She could face neither Armand nor Céline after this. She had no wish to confront them with their crime. The crime was her father's also. The stupidity was her own. She packed at once, not giving much thought to how she would leave until she stood and looked at her cases. Then she took a deep breath and went to find Mathilde. She would have to do some deceiving herself.

On Monday morning Sarah stood and surveyed the shop. It was no consolation and brought no happiness, but it was hers and nobody could touch that. Here, she was secure and she glanced with affection at Dulcie who had come in this morning to bring her up to date on things and hand the business back over to her.

It seemed ages since Friday, since she had raced home to England and tried to shake off the misery of her time with Armand. It had been remarkably easy to deceive Mathilde. She had readily believed the story that Sarah had an emergency in London. She had even organised a taxi all the way to Paris.

Dulcie had not been deceived at all. She had known about the promise and she knew Sarah well enough to know that her promises were not broken lightly. It was too soon, too raw, to tell her anything but she had taken one look at Sarah and invited her to stay for the weekend.

'You shouldn't be alone,' she had stated firmly when Sarah had protested that she would be no sort of pleasant company. 'This is no time for you to be going back to that house with all its memories.'

And it was not. The memories now were clouded. Her father had not acted as she had expected and he seemed to have been a different man from the one she remembered. It had taken very little persuasion to get her to go to Dulcie's bright flat and spend the weekend there. She had to get back into her own life now, though. She had to put everything behind her and she knew it would not be an easy task.

'Here's your favourite customer,' Dulcie whispered as an old man came into the shop, his face lighting up at the sight of Sarah. 'He's been haunting the place with a parcel under his arm since you left. He wouldn't trade with me.'

'He looks for books for me. It's his hobby,' Sarah murmured. 'I'll have to deal with him.'

'Well, I'll be off.' Dulcie kissed her cheek. 'Come and stay tonight too, Sarah. You don't look any happier.'

'I'll be all right,' Sarah assured her with a slight smile. 'One day, I'll tell you about it.'

'Just ring if you need me,' Dulcie said softly. She hugged Sarah impulsively and then left, nodding cheerfully to the old man who was waiting with an eager expression on his face. Sarah walked out into the shop, making herself smile. She had no enthusiasm at all now but she would have to get some; she would have to go back to being the person she was before she met Armand.

'Mr Gresham! How lovely to see you.' Sarah gave him a beaming smile and the man's old face relaxed into joy as he put the parcel down on the counter with the air of a magician.

'Look what I found, Miss Thorpe!' he exclaimed. 'It's a first edition; I'm almost sure!'

They were both eagerly browsing through the book when another customer came in but neither of them looked up. Sarah had a magnifying glass on the flyleaf of the book and they were excitedly examining the few scrawled words there.

'How much did you pay for it?' she asked and he laughed in a gleeful manner.

'Forty. I felt like a criminal.'

'You're just an expert,' Sarah corrected him firmly. 'I'll give you a hundred if you want to sell.'

'I thought I'd give it to you as a gift,' Mr Gresham told her seriously. 'You're good to me, Miss Thorpe.'

'I appreciate you.' Sarah smiled. 'You find me all sorts of things that I would never have the time to look for. I consider you to be an asset and I won't take any fights. One hundred or I won't even look at it any more.'

'You're a tough little thing,' he muttered and then he smiled, back to glee. 'I'm going to Bath next week. See what I get there and we'll settle up later?'

'Fine.' Sarah straightened up and smiled again. 'I wish I could go with you.'

'I would be proud,' he said gallantly. 'You've got my card. If you want to go, just ring me.'

'I will.' Sarah shook hands with him and then turned to the new customer as Mr Gresham made his way to the door.

Her whole body started in shock and it was a few seconds before she could pull herself together. She could not see who had come into the shop because he was behind the end bookcase, looking through the books. Only the top of his head was visible but it was the darkness of the hair, the thick shine of it and something about the way he held his head... For a moment she had thought it was Armand and now Sarah turned to the back of the shop, hurrying into the small room where she made her lunch when she was here.

She leaned against the wall once she was safely inside. Her legs were shaking, her heart pounding and she felt the beginning of tears pricking at her eyes. Just at the sight of a dark head! She would have to get a better grip on herself because she could not go around imagining she saw Armand in everyone. Thousands of men had thick dark hair, thousands of men were tall and powerful. Was she going to feel panic-stricken and faint at the sight of every one of them?

She took a few deep breaths and walked back into the shop, her face still pale, but it paled even more as she saw the man standing by the door. He was turning the sign to 'closed' and pulling down the door-blind, and this time her heart was not playing tricks.

'Armand!' She whispered the name and he turned, his dark eyes lancing over her.

'Hello, *chérie*,' he said softly. 'I am just making sure that you do not run away again.'

Sarah stared at him, unable to move; her legs were trembling badly and she wanted to sit down but she could not even do that. Armand stood and looked at her and he said nothing at all for a long time; then he said quietly, 'I have come for you, Sarah. Do you wish to talk here or would you prefer to take me to your house? We can, of course, go to my hotel but I would not want to be in polite company should you decide to aim one of your blows at me because this time I may very well put you over my knee and spank you.'

'I—I don't think we have anything to say to each other,' Sarah managed stiffly through trembling lips. 'I know all I need to know. One day perhaps I'll be able to laugh at it. One day it might even seem to have been a good idea, but right now I can only think of how everyone made a fool of me.'

Armand watched her quietly and then he nodded in understanding and her heart sank even lower. He was not going to deny it. Why was he here? Surely they didn't think she would go back now, keep to her promise when she knew everything?

'I know how you feel,' he agreed softly. 'You were tricked to some extent. You do not have the full story, though. That is why I am here. I came to tell you...'

'Well, I don't want to know!' Sarah snapped, coming out of her miserable trance and turning abruptly away from him. 'You both did what you had to do, you and Céline. Now leave me alone!'

'I did not have to make love to you. I swore from the first that I would have nothing to do with this but you drew me into it, you with your fair hair, your tilted blue eyes and your utter innocence.'

'I'm not innocent now, am I?' Sarah cried bitterly, spinning round to face him. He was closer than she had expected and he stood looking down into her unhappy, accusing eyes. He smiled slowly.

'You are not a virgin,' he corrected her quietly, 'but oh, you are innocent, Sarah.' He looked round impatiently and then reached for her coat. 'Come. I wish to talk to you privately. We will leave here before some other old man comes to dote on you like a grandfather and offer to give you a valuable book.'

'I can't just close the shop,' Sarah protested unevenly. But she was making no effort to resist as Armand held her coat and firmly placed her bag in her hands. She would have to resist! Whatever he wanted to say it was

going to be more lies, more efforts to get her back to
France and out of London.

'The shop is already closed,' he reminded her firmly.
'Staying here is pointless because if any customers arrive
I will fiercely see them off.'

'I'm in London!' Sarah pointed out sharply, her
temper beginning to rise. 'I'm safe here.'

'And soon you will be in France,' he informed her as
he opened the door and ushered her outside. 'You will
be safer there because I will be with you.'

'Look . . . !' Sarah began frostily but he never even
glanced at her. He was busy locking the door.

'Later I will look,' he insisted calmly. 'Now we will
drive to your house. I have a car parked here. I hired
it.'

Before she knew it, Sarah had been bundled into a
grey car that was parked by the kerb; Armand never
asked directions—he simply drove out into the traffic
and headed for her own home.

'You know where I live?' Sarah asked in a whisper
and he nodded with satisfaction.

'Naturally, Céline had your address. In any case, I
certainly should know where you live; I have been parked
on the doorstep almost all the time since Saturday
morning. I have left only to sleep at my hotel. The rest
of my time has been spent between a closed bookshop
and an empty house. I have lived on beefburgers and
hot dogs, sandwiches and cold tea. You have a lot to
answer for, *ma belle*, and if I develop a stomach injury
I will hold you entirely responsible.'

Sarah was silent. He was so sure of himself, so sure
of her! She was still silent as they stopped at the house
she had called home since childhood. She had not been
back in there since she returned. Even her suitcases were
still at Dulcie's flat. This was not like home any more
because her father was not as she had imagined.

'I—I can't go in there,' she said in a low, unhappy voice and Armand glanced sharply at her.

'You can and you will,' he insisted. 'Before this day is over you will know he loved you and how much he loved you. No one in the future will be able to make you uneasy with lies. Come, Sarah; open the door. There is nothing to fear from the past and nothing to make you unhappy about the future.'

She went in because she had to, but her eyes slid away from the picture of her father, a large framed photograph that stood on the side-table in the drawing-room. She was with her father in the photograph. He had his arm round her and they were both laughing at the camera. Those had been happy days, days when her world was bright.

'So, this is John Thorpe?' Armand said softly, taking the photograph in his hand and looking at it for a long time. 'John Thorpe and his beloved daughter.'

Sarah's breath snatched in her throat and she turned away but Armand took her arm and held her fast.

'I have a letter,' he said quietly. 'You will read this and it will explain more than I could ever do in a short time.'

He handed it to her and she saw her father's handwriting. She also saw the name and address and looked up with shocked eyes.

'This is to Céline! I can't read her letters!'

'She wishes it,' Armand told her firmly. 'She gave it to me in order that you could read it and I insist. If you do not, I will read it aloud. It would be better to read it for yourself.'

She looked up into his implacable face and knew that there was no getting out of this. When Armand decided something it would be done, no matter who objected. He paced about as she sat and read the letter and the first few words were enough to have her looking up with distressed eyes.

'It—it's a love letter,' she said desperately.

'More than you know,' he returned softly, stopping to look down at her. 'I have read it, also at Céline's insistence. read it all, Sarah.'

He turned away again and Sarah read, her teeth nibbling at her lips. She was not embarrassed—it was too beautiful for that—but she felt like an intruder, someone breaking in on the wonderful thing that had been between her father and Céline—especially now, when she felt more distant from her father than she had felt all her life.

Gradually, her trembling stopped; her eyes slowly read the letter, savouring every word, and when she had finished she looked up to see Armand watching her with a look of tenderness on his face.

'It is a letter of love to two women,' he told her quietly. 'It is to the two women who were his life: Céline and his own precious daughter. And what does he say, *chérie*, that would make you doubt him? It is true that he wanted Céline to have you at the château for a month and it is true that he wanted you to forget this man in London, but his last words were that if you could not, then he would be content to let you go to somebody he disliked and mistrusted. "Her happiness is everything to me." That is what he wrote, Sarah.'

There were tears in her eyes and she turned her head to look at the man she had lost, the man she had thought had let her down.

'Oh, Daddy!' Tears fell fast and she had no resistance when Armand strode across to clasp her in his arms.

'Your happiness is what he wanted, Sarah,' Armand reminded her softly. 'Come back to me and be happy.'

'How can I when you've got Violette?' She looked up at him with brimming eyes. 'I came back because she told me—she told me that...'

'I know what she told you,' he said. 'Why do you think I am here? Why do you think I came for you instead of staying in Paris and cursing myself for imagining that you loved me? I told Violette nothing, *chérie*. She had her information from that old gossip Mathilde who listened in when Céline and I were arguing about you. I did not want you to come to France. I thought it disgraceful and my mother and I had several spats before I came to Paris to pick you up. Mathilde heard one of those arguments and told Violette.'

Sarah searched his face and found only the truth, and his hand wiped the tears from her cheeks as he smiled into her eyes.

'I am glad you came to the château,' he whispered, burying his face in her cloudy hair. 'Otherwise I would never have known what it is to love.'

Sarah drew back to look at him and he cupped her face in his hands gently.

'I love you, *petite*,' he said unevenly. 'I suppose I have loved you since that first night in the storm when I looked up and you were drifting down the stairs, so beautiful, so innocent. And when I lifted you and your body settled so closely to mine, I knew then that one day you would belong to me.'

'But why did Mathilde tell Violette?' Sarah wanted to know, holding back her joy for the time being to dispel every last cloud on the horizon.

'Mathilde likes you, admires you, and you already know how delicate she imagines you to be. To Mathilde it was a disgrace that you were being kept against your will.'

'Against my will?' Sarah looked startled and Armand grinned down at her.

'Mathilde has more imagination than intelligence,' he admitted. 'She also imagined that Violette would one day be my wife. She was therefore only sharing her knowledge with the family. She felt quite justified.'

'How do you know all this?' Sarah asked breathlessly as his arms tightened around her.

'When I discovered that you were gone and heard your fairy-tale to Mathilde, I phoned my mother who came back like a black whirlwind.' He began to laugh. 'You do not know your future mother-in-law, *chérie*,' he assured her softly. 'She was determined to get to the bottom of all the mystery and after a few moments in the quiet of the kitchen Mathilde was in tears and had confessed her crime. One call to Violette cleared things up completely.'

'Did Céline phone Violette?' Sarah asked and he smiled down at her rather grimly.

'No. I did that myself. I had to let her know that I would be marrying you as soon as possible. I would hate to look a fool, so... when will you marry me, my sweet Sarah?'

'Armand, do you really mean it?' She looked up at him with starry eyes and he swept her into his arms, moving to sit down and settling her on his lap.

'I would have asked you when I came back from Paris if you had not run away,' he told her, beginning to plant fierce kisses on her face and neck. 'I would also have explained about your father's wish to protect you from this—this...'

'Jerk?' Sarah enquired and Armand's English was good enough to encompass that.

'For want of a more indelicate word that will do,' he growled. He gasped with pleasure when she threw her arms around his neck. 'Beautiful, beautiful Sarah,' he murmured. He smiled down at her. 'My prickly English rose, my own little innocent.'

'I'm not innocent now,' Sarah reminded him with colour flooding her cheeks and his hand stroked her skin gently.

'I took your virginity,' he admitted huskily, 'but not your innocence. I never wish to see that go. It is the shine in your eyes, the belief you have in people, your gentle loving ways. You have left the château in desolation, my love. Come back with me and never leave again. We will spare Céline time. We will visit her on many weekends and she will also stay with us in Paris. And one day soon she will feel much closer to your father because they will have something together, a grandchild to share.'

Tears came back into Sarah's eyes and he held her tenderly.

'Do not cry, my darling,' he whispered softly into her hair. 'Céline remembers with happiness. We will give her a grandchild to love. We will unite them when they could not be united before.'

'Oh, I love you, Armand,' she cried, hugging him close, and he smiled against her face.

'I know it. I knew that wonderful night when you gave yourself to me so sweetly. You will have all your life to prove it and I will prove my love too.'

His lips closed over hers and Sarah relaxed into the happiness he had brought. The house was peaceful again, her old home, a place she would never sell. Nobody would ever live here unless they were family. Céline would stay here as often as she liked and one day they would have a Christmas here, all of them, and her father would know.

'Family,' she whispered against his lips and Armand caught her even closer.

'Family,' he agreed tenderly. 'Lots of children to race around the château, to ride the horses and come to England and stay in this house with their grandmother.'

'You understand me,' Sarah acknowledged softly as his lips trailed over her slender neck.

'I adore you,' he whispered. 'I think I have understood you since I first saw you standing bewildered and anxious at the airport. From that moment I wanted to protect you but I fought against it. I imagined you loved this man in London.'

'But I never did,' Sarah protested. 'I never for one moment thought of it. It was just that he had me in a turmoil, more or less in his clutches.'

'Never again,' Armand muttered, kissing her fiercely.

'He never tried to come back,' Sarah mused. 'I wonder if he...?'

'I do not think so,' Armand murmured drily, standing and pulling her to her feet. 'I advised him against it. I threatened him, very pleasantly. He was much impressed.'

'I believe you,' Sarah assured him, looking up at him with wide, wary eyes.

'And do you believe me when I tell you that I want you badly?' he asked thickly, his ironical look dying away. 'I have waited with unbelievable patience since I came to London, but now we are alone and there is no reason to wait any longer.'

'If I asked you to wait until we're married...' Sarah began, and he looked at her with love in his eyes.

'I would wait, *chérie.*'

'But I'm not going to ask you,' she confessed, laughing into his suddenly mournful face, and he swept her up into his arms.

'Terrible things happen to those who tease,' he threatened as his lips possessively covered hers.

Sarah sat with Céline in the garden. It was late summer, more than a year since Sarah had first come to the dark château. It was not dark now. The sun was hot and the

sky brilliantly blue. Their eyes were happily on Armand,
who walked by the gurgling stream with his son, the
cuddly, dark-haired boy held high in his arms.

'I'm so happy, Céline,' Sarah said softly and Céline
turned to her with a smile.

'I know, *ma chère*,' she answered. 'You were always
happy with Armand, right from the first. I used to watch
you together and I knew my dreams would come true:
my son and John's daughter. After your trip to Paris I
knew for sure. The air sang when you were close to each
other. I could have killed Mathilde. I thought she had
spoiled everything. Armand was white and shaken,
desolate, but I was in a great rage.'

'Armand told me.' Sarah laughed. 'Mathilde seems to
be happy now, though.'

'Oh, she is a good soul,' Céline admitted generously.
'She is easy to please. From time to time I allow her to
bully me and she adores Jean-Pierre, as you can see.'

'Don't we all?' Sarah sighed happily, watching
Armand talking intently to his son.

'You think he is a little like John?' Céline asked wist-
fully and Sarah's hand covered hers at once.

'Just like him,' she agreed softly. 'Last night when we
put him to bed, Armand and I were watching him for
a long time and we both agreed that there's a lot of my
father in him.'

Armand came back and handed the laughing child to
his grandmother who eagerly took him off to see the
horses.

'There is a happy lady, *chérie*,' Armand said quietly,
pulling Sarah to her feet and folding her in his arms.
'When we go back to Paris I think she will want to come
too. We will have to buy a house there now, one big
enough for a family.'

Sarah rested her head on his broad shoulder as he
stroked her hair.

'She wanted to know if he was like my father and I told her that we thought so,' she said softly.

'And he is,' Armand agreed. 'So will they all be. It is a love that will just go on and on forever.' He tilted her face up to her and looked down into her eyes. 'But I still think they should have married. I cannot bear to think of a night without you in my arms or of a day when I cannot look forward to seeing your lovely face.'

'We've done what we could to make things right for them,' Sarah whispered, reaching up to kiss him, and he smiled down at her, gathering her tightly to him.

'And we will go on making things right, my own,' he murmured against her lips. 'We will make sure that wherever Céline turns there will be a face that looks like her John, hmm?'

'It's a big project,' Sarah laughed.

'But you are capable of it,' he murmured seductively. 'You will sell your bookshop and settle down to being merely my wife? You will give it some thought?'

'I have thought,' Sarah whispered. 'I'll let the smaller venture go and tackle the bigger enterprise.'

Armand was laughing as his lips covered hers and, in the kitchen, Mathilde went back to stirring her delicious concoction for dinner, a smile on her face, her spying well worthwhile.

'*C'est belle*!' she murmured to herself. '*La vie, c'est merveilleuse*!'

HARLEQUIN ROMANCE®

brings you:

A letter has played an important role in all our romances in our Sealed with a Kiss series so far, and next month's WANTED: WIFE AND MOTHER by Barbara McMahon is no exception.

But for Caroline Evans, the letter from Australian rancher Nick Silverman comes as something of a shock. His letter isn't sealed with a kiss—it's a coldhearted proposal! Nick needs a mother to take care of his little orphaned niece, Amanda. And Caroline needs to marry to fulfill the conditions of her great-aunt's will. A marriage of convenience seems an ideal solution for all three of them but, with a cynical and sexy stranger for a husband, has Caroline taken on more than she can handle?

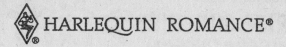

HARLEQUIN ROMANCE®

brings you

Romances that take the family to heart!

Harlequin Romance #3370
MAKE-BELIEVE MARRIAGE by RENEE ROSZEL

To ease her grandfather Otis's mind, Mercy Stewart had told a little white lie. Well, quite a big white lie really, but it was one she was beginning to regret. He longed to see her settled down, and telling him she had married Damon DeMorney seemed to solve all her problems. Otis was overjoyed! Unfortunately, her make-believe spouse had also learned of the change to his bachelor status: Damon was furious! But then he thought of a way to turn the situation to his advantage. If Mercy had told everyone she was his wife, then that's what she would be—and as far as he was concerned, that opened up all sorts of interesting possibilities!

Available in July wherever Harlequin books are sold.

ANNOUNCING THE

PRISE SURPRISE SWEEPSTAKES!

This month's prize:

L-A-R-G-E—SCREEN PANASONIC TV!

This month, as a special surprise, we're giving away a fabulous FREE TV!

Imagine how delighted you and your family will be to own this brand-new 31" Panasonic** television! It comes with all the latest high-tech features, like a SuperFlat picture tube for a clear, crisp picture...unified remote control...closed-caption decoder...clock and sleep timer, and much more!

The facing page contains two Entry Coupons (as does every book you received this shipment). Complete and return *all* the entry coupons; **the more times you enter, the better your chances of winning the TV!**

Then keep your fingers crossed, because you'll find out by July 15, 1995 if you're the winner!

Remember: The more times you enter, the better your chances of winning!*